People of the Sacred Arrows

People of the Sacred Arrows

The Southern Cheyenne Today

▽ ▽ ▽ ▽ ▽ ▽ ▽ ▽ ▽ ▽ ▽

Stan Hoig

Illustrated with photographs and old prints

COBBLEHILL BOOKS
Dutton   New York

PHOTOGRAPH CREDITS

© Keith Ball, 104 (top); Courtesy of Lawrence Hart, 10; Stan
Hoig, 7, 12, 24, 31, 33, 41, 46, 49, 51, 56, 57, 58, 61, 69, 72,
83, 84, 85, 87, 92, 93, 96, 97, 99; Oklahoma Historical Society,
Archives and Manuscripts Division, 27, 36–37, courtesy of Terry
Zinn, 104 (bottom); Courtesy of John Sipes, Jr., 119; Smithsonian Institution, National Anthropological Archives, 5, 22, 65, 76,
117, DeLancey Gill, Bureau of Ethnology Collection, 79; State
Historical Society of Colorado, 20; University of Oklahoma Library, Western History Collection, 66–67, 110–111.

Library of Congress Cataloging-in-Publication Data
Hoig, Stan.
People of the sacred arrows : the Southern Cheyenne today /
Stan Hoig.
    p.   cm.
Includes bibliographical references (p.   ) and index.
Summary: Depicts the background, beliefs, and past and present
way of life of the Southern Cheyennes.
ISBN 0-525-65088-1
1. Cheyenne Indians—Juvenile literature.   [1. Cheyenne Indians.
2. Indians of North America.]   I. Title.
E99.C53H64   1992
976.6′004973—dc20   91-44428   CIP   AC

Published in the United States by Cobblehill Books, an affiliate of
Dutton Children's Books, a division of Penguin Books USA Inc.,
375 Hudson Street, New York, New York 10014

Designed by Mina Greenstein
Printed in the United States of America
First Edition   10 9 8 7 6 5 4 3 2 1

This book is dedicated
to the memory of
RANDY ROMAN NOSE
who, before his untimely death,
had dreamed of one day leading his people
as
Tribal Chairman

Contents

Foreword

THIS BOOK is primarily about the Southern Cheyenne. It must be noted, however, that much of what is said about them and their hardships is also true of the Southern Arapaho. The two tribes have been interrelated for many years, and a good amount of intermarriage has taken place. They are bound together by common problems, a common government, and the commonality of being Indian.

The Northern Cheyenne and Northern Arapaho, on the other hand, have not been so interassociated, the former residing on their reservation in Montana and the latter being located in the Wind River region of northern Wyoming.

The Southern Cheyenne and Southern Arapaho still clearly distinguish themselves as separate people. Both have their own native language, their own traditions, their own chiefs and cultural leaders, and their own religious ceremonies.

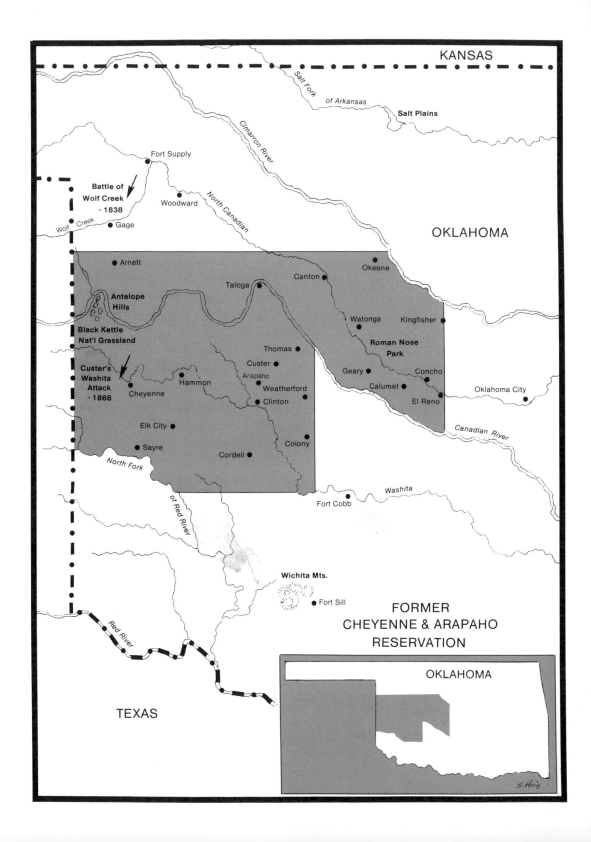

Walter Hamilton, who is half-Cheyenne and half-Arapaho, explained why he could not speak either native tongue. The reason, he said, was that his parents were both very stubborn people. His father, a Cheyenne chief, would speak Cheyenne in asking for things at the table. His mother would answer only in Arapaho. As a result, the one language the family had in common was English.

The Southern Arapaho attend their own Arapaho Sun Dance in Wyoming during July each year and do not participate in the Southern Cheyenne Sun Dance or Sacred Medicine Arrow Renewal held in Oklahoma in June. Though there is general harmony between the two tribes, there is a degree of competition. Some members of both tribes have expressed a desire to be legally separated, but in the face of great political, economic, and social difficulty, this action does not seem likely.

In writing this book I have worked to tell the Southern Cheyenne story essentially as it has been revealed to me by Cheyennes, by observation, and through other sources. Having heretofore written about the Cheyenne largely in their historical abstract, preparing this book has offered me a rewarding experience in meeting and knowing a generous, hospitable, and gracious people.

I was raised on Wolf Creek in northwestern Oklahoma just north of the Cheyenne and Arapaho reservation area. Historically, this was "Indian country," though as a boy I knew little of its past. I recall with great affection, however, the small-but-perfect arrowhead I once found while crossing a rivulet. It left me wondering if perhaps an Indian boy of my own age may have left it there.

Like many Oklahomans, I grew up within the sphere of white society oblivious to Indian people, their history, and their culture. It is especially rewarding now to see the fuller picture of the original inhabitants of western Oklahoma, a part of the world for which

I, too, have great affection. I feel I have learned much from the experience.

I am especially grateful to John Sipes, Jr., and his wife, Dee; Quentin Roman Nose of Watonga Mid-high; and Darrell Rice of the *Watonga Republican* for their counsel, advice, and guidance. For the most part, the newspapers in western Oklahoma give scant attention to the affairs of the Cheyenne and other Indian tribes. The *Republican*, which covers the business and social affairs of Cheyennes and Arapahos in great detail, has been a noteworthy exception.

I would hope two things for this book: that it helps non-Indians understand the injustices which the Cheyenne and other Indian people have suffered historically and still endure today; and that it encourages all young Indians to be self-prideful and live a worthy life, however they wish to define it.

Theirs is a song of the soul, crying.
The words are silent like the dead, staring.
No one hears but those who have the song.

—S.H.

People of the
Sacred Arrows

▷ 1 ◁

A Dilemma of Culture

Tommy Magpie sat staring at his American history book. He read a few lines about the Minutemen at Concord, Massachusetts, but the book failed to hold his interest. His mind was on a story he had heard told many times at home. It was about how as a boy his ancestor, Cheyenne Chief Magpie, had fought against the blue-coat soldiers who attacked his village on Lodge Pole River, the stream in western Oklahoma that white people call the Washita.

Tommy imagined himself in Chief Black Kettle's camp. He had just been awakened by the crack of gunfire. Dashing for the lodge opening, he saw his father crumple to the ground with a hard grunt, his rifle unfired and his red blood staining the snow. Then Tommy saw the wall of horsemen charging from across the river into the camp.

As the cavalrymen fired their pistols and swung their long

knives at the terrified villagers who were trying to flee their tipis, the boy could hear the screaming of women and children. One of the horsemen headed directly for Tommy, and he quickly grabbed his father's rifle and ran to take refuge in the bottom of a small ravine.

Peering over the rim of the ravine, he saw a man wearing the insignia of a blue-coat officer riding toward him on a brown horse. Tommy leveled the heavy gun, took aim, and pulled the trigger. The gun exploded its shot, and when the smoke cleared Tommy saw the brown horse galloping away, the rider no longer on its back. He did not know if the man was dead or not, but there were no more bullets for the rifle. He had no choice but to head on downstream to where the other Cheyenne villages were camped. Perhaps there he could help fight the blue-coats who had killed his father and massacred his village.

SUDDENLY TOMMY heard his teacher talking, scolding him for not paying attention in class. His classmates were looking at him, laughing.

"I guess you're just not very interested in history, Tommy," his teacher commented dryly.

Embarrassed, he ducked his head. He was very interested in history—but history that related to him and his world. Somehow he felt cheated. The history books did not tell how U.S. troops massacred a peaceful village of Cheyenne Indians on November 27, 1868. One of the best-remembered incidents of history to Cheyennes is the attack on Black Kettle's camp on the Washita River by General George Armstrong Custer and the U.S. 7th Cavalry.

The Minutemen at Concord were heroes for defending their

Chief Magpie, only a youngster at the time, helped fight Custer's troops when his village on the Washita was attacked by surprise.

land against invaders, Tommy thought. But nothing like that is ever said about the Indian warriors who fought and died to protect their land and their homes. Somehow, this didn't seem fair.

To most non-Indian Americans, Custer's attack at the Washita is viewed as a part of the romantic history of the old West. The Cheyenne, however, regard it as one of the bitterest episodes in their long and continuing abuse at the hands of the United States government, army, and citizenry. To the Cheyenne, even today, Custer symbolizes white injustice and aggression.

Southern Cheyenne youths, like Tommy, too often feel that they are being excluded by the world around them. Living in and around small towns in western Oklahoma, they go to schools in which most students are white. Their skins are darker, and that bothers some people. Some white parents tell their children that Indians are lazy, and they should not mix with them.

In turn, Cheyenne parents tell their children that they should not associate with such people. Again and again they tell them: you are Cheyenne, and the Cheyennes are a proud people. But young Indians like Tommy find it very difficult to feel proud when others look down on them and fail to show ordinary human respect.

"Almost all of the great men the history books tell about are white men," observed Mrs. Mercy Haag, who tutors Indian children at Calumet, Oklahoma. "They do not talk about men like Black Kettle or White Antelope or Lean Bear. These were all brave men who were killed while trying to make peace with the white man.

"At school, Indian children are told that they should be like white people, that they should work hard so they can become wealthy. But striving to possess things and becoming rich is not the Indian way. To Cheyennes, the most important things are inner strength and values such as honesty and generosity."

The Cheyenne value system is taught through long-held traditions and tribal beliefs. These teachings are much the same as those of Christianity, based on love and respect for one another.

This granite marker overlooks the site of Custer's attack on Black Kettle's Cheyenne village at the Washita.

Why then, young Cheyennes wonder, is it so wrong in the eyes of white people to be Cheyenne?

Before the white man came, the Cheyenne roamed in great freedom over the plains of central North America. Then there were no roads, no towns, and no fences. But there were abundant herds of wild game, especially the buffalo upon which the Indians of the Plains existed. Then the soldiers came and drove the Cheyenne and their confederated tribe, the Arapaho, onto a reservation that was established in 1869 on a part of their former range in western Oklahoma.

There the government tried to make farmers and stock raisers out of the former hunters of the prairie, but the programs were never very successful. Then the government decided it was necessary to destroy the tribal system altogether. And after a few years it gave in to the great public clamor to open up the Indian lands to non-Indian settlement. Indian leaders resisted, making their views heard in Washington, D.C., but to no avail.

"The Great Spirit gave the Indian all this country," Cheyenne Chief Old Crow argued at the time, "and never tell them that they should sell it. I am poor. I have no money. I don't want money; money doesn't do an Indian any good. Here is my wealth, the earth. Here is all the wealth I want, the only money I know how to keep."

The Cheyenne and Arapaho people were forced to take individual allotments. Each family was assigned either 80 acres for farmland or 160 acres for grazing, upon which they were required to reside. They were thus forced to live apart from one another, rather than together as a tribal unit. Later, most of their remaining reservation was opened to the general population, and settlers flooded in like swarming bees.

Today the Southern Cheyenne and Southern Arapaho continue to reside in their former reservation area, though few still live on the family allotments. Most of them are clustered in and about the small farming towns of western Oklahoma—towns that had sprung up when the white settlers moved in. Though the two tribes have held fiercely to their tribal traditions and identity, their long exposure to American society has, inevitably, wrought changes upon them and their way of life.

As do other Indians, the Cheyennes face a crucial dilemma. It poses the question: how can they retain their tribal culture, which is the essence of their being as a people, and at the same time live in harmony with modern American society?

"We are becoming more and more fearful," worried one Cheyenne leader, "that our tribal culture will be run over. The modern world goes too fast. Everyone is hurrying around to make money. We don't want our young people to forget the basic, good things in life."

In the past it has been government policy to try to change the Indian and make him into the likeness of the Anglo-American. This program has failed badly. Most American Indian tribes have been left to exist as impoverished minorities amidst dominant white communities which, for the most part, condemn the Indian for being Indian.

Educated people among the Southern Cheyenne are attempting to deal with their dilemma. Indian leaders have come to realize the value of political power in securing justice and economic relief.

They are defying the government axiom that white is necessarily better. They feel that by knowing and experiencing their own tribal traditions their children will develop the confidence and self-assurance they need to compete in the school or workplace.

Cheyenne Chief Lawrence Hart, a former U.S. Marine Corps jet pilot who resides in Clinton, Oklahoma, has been working to help Indian children find identity and meaning to their lives by learning more of their history and culture.

"Self and tribal identity are prerequisite to the building of esteem in our youth," Chief Hart observes. "Our children must know who they are if they are to find success in life. The unfortunate truth is that, either unintentionally or unknowingly,

Cheyenne Chief Lawrence Hart served with the U.S. Marines as a jet fighter pilot.

most public schools teach majority history almost exclusively.

"This tends to propagate racial biases. It is psychologically damaging to Indian children to be taught by inference that their past is negative and their race is somehow inferior."

Quentin Roman Nose, Indian counselor at Watonga, Oklahoma, Mid-high School, is also deeply engaged in an effort to build the self-esteem of young Indians. He himself suffered the trauma of an Indian youth growing up in a white-dominated society. He has seen firsthand how damage to personal spirit can result in problems of school dropout, alcoholism, drugs, suicide, and social violence.

"Many Indian boys and girls," he agrees sadly, "suffer from an identity crisis. They grow up in communities where the general perception of Indian people is negative. This leaves them caught in limbo, neither white nor truly Indian. It is very difficult for them."

Only time will tell what the effect will be on the Southern Cheyennes' efforts to restore and elevate tribal heritage among their young. It can be hoped that it will produce a generation of Tommy Magpies who will find a happy and worthwhile adjustment of their tribal being with the modern world—and that from these will spring educated, capable leaders for tomorrow.

This bust of Cheyenne Chief Black Kettle by Gregory Perillo was presented to the Cheyenne and Arapaho tribes by the state of Oklahoma.

2

Black Kettle,
the Great Peacemaker

ON SEPTEMBER 19, 1990, a ceremony was held in the rotunda of the Oklahoma State Capitol at Oklahoma City to unveil a life-sized bust of the famed Cheyenne Principal Chief, Black Kettle. The act commemorated one of America's great Indian leaders who died while trying to bring about harmony between his people and the whites.

The bust, valued at $36,000, was a gift from the state of Oklahoma to the Southern Cheyenne and Arapaho tribes.

Over three hundred persons crowded the rotunda. They included some forty descendants of Black Kettle, Cheyenne-Arapaho tribal leaders, dignitaries, and other guests. The oldest member of the Black Kettle family was eighty-three-year-old Jenny Black Pendleton, a great-granddaughter of the famous chief.

The program was opened with traditional Indian flute music, and Chief Lawrence Hart served as the master of ceremonies. After the invocation, flag song, and presentation of colors, Governor Henry Bellmon spoke on the advancement that has been made in bringing harmony between the Indian and white races in Oklahoma. It was a message of tribute to the Indian population of the state.

"It is important to the entire state of Oklahoma," the governor observed, "that our cultural and ethnic heritage be remembered, protected, and passed on to our young people."

A brief history of the Southern Cheyenne was then presented, noting in particular the exceptional peace efforts of Black Kettle. He had tried his best to live in harmony with the whites who had flooded onto the Cheyenne homeland and hunting grounds during the nineteenth century. Kansas Indian trader James R. Mead, who knew Black Kettle well, once stated:

"Black Kettle was not a hostile and never had been; his boast was that his hand had never been raised against a white man, woman, or child. He was a mild, peaceable, pleasant, good man."

Cheyenne Chief Rollin Haag introduced Gregory Perillo of New York, sculptor of the Black Kettle bust. Together, the two men removed the colorful Pendleton blanket, a favorite among Indians, from the bronze image of Black Kettle. The bust was then blessed by Cheyenne Sun Dance priest William Bent Fletcher of Geary, Oklahoma. Willie, who is also a Cheyenne headman, is a descendent of the well-known, half-blood frontiersman, George Bent.

Tribal Chairperson Juanita L. Learned, an Arapaho, expressed the thanks of the Cheyenne-Arapaho Tribe for the precious gift, ending the ceremony. The Black Kettle bust has since been placed on permanent display in the tribal government headquarters at Concho, near El Reno, Oklahoma.

"In truth, the bust represents more than just one man," Chief Hart noted. "It is emblematic of the Cheyenne as a people and exemplifies the many great Indian chiefs of American history.

"The historical role of the Cheyenne chief is often misunderstood. His principal role was not to lead in war, as many think, but to maintain peace within and without the tribe. The chief was a peacemaker in the tradition of our cultural hero Sweet Medicine."

"A good chief," one Cheyenne historian noted, "gave his whole heart and his whole mind to the work of helping his people, and strove for their welfare with an earnestness rarely equaled by the rulers of other men."

Efforts are being made by the Cheyennes to bring attention to some of their great leaders of their past. These were men whose lives illustrate high courage, integrity, and dedication to the cause of peace. A number of them, like Black Kettle, forfeited their lives in that cause.

Black Kettle, like most Cheyenne chiefs, had been a warrior as a young man, carrying out the warrior's role of provider and protector for his people. But upon reaching his mature years, as was common with most Cheyenne chiefs, his role changed drastically. Now he became a father to the tribal body. He exercised a spirit of good will and benevolent wisdom that became reflected in his eyes and overall countenance.

Black Kettle's life paralleled and was deeply involved in the period of white conquest of the Central Plains of America. It was during this period that the Cheyenne nation rose to greatness and then suffered betrayal and defeat at the hands of the United States military.

Black Kettle was a young teen-ager when the Cheyennes met their first American military expedition on the Missouri River in

1825. Like other tribesmen, he watched in awe when the soldiers fired their rockets across the wide channel of the Missouri to impress the Indians.

The Cheyenne Principal Chief at the time was High-Backed Wolf, or Wolf-on-the-Hill. He is believed by some to have been Black Kettle's father. The journalist of the Atkinson party was greatly impressed with the chief, writing:

"He is one of the most dignified and elegant-looking men I ever saw."

The famous Indian artist George Catlin, who painted both High-Backed Wolf and his comely wife, She-Who-Bathes-Her-Knees, was similarly impressed. He described the chief as one of the noblest Indians he had ever met. Traders, too, lauded him as a man of high honor and integrity.

When the tribe was first encountered in Minnesota by French traders, Indians lived by hunting small game and cultivating corn. Being a small tribe and residing in fixed villages, they were often ravaged by the mass attacks of Assiniboines and Crees from Canada. The Cheyenne attempted to escape by moving into southeastern North Dakota. Archaeological evidence indicates that their villages were overrun there as well.

Again the Cheyenne fled, this time moving south of the Missouri River to the region of the Black Hills of South Dakota. They now became allied with the Arapaho, who spoke the same Algonquian tongue. The Arapahos fought with them against enemy tribes.

It was here during the last half of the eighteenth century that two significant factors affected great change upon the Cheyenne. They discovered the enormous benefit of hunting among the great herds of buffalo that grazed up and down the Central Plains of

North America. At first they hunted the animal on foot by the "surround" method. An entire band would fan out and drive a herd of buffalo into a trap or off a cliff.

Also during this time, the Spanish horse, which had multiplied on the grassy ranges of the southern prairies, arrived in the north. The horse had a great influence on all the Plains tribes, but none more so than the Cheyenne. Now the tribe could reside in buffalo-hide tipis and move from place to place, making them far less vulnerable to surprise attack.

The horse also provided their men new dimensions of mobility and range. The Cheyenne warrior soon earned the reputation of a fierce combatant in battle, one who could ride far and fast to strike back at his enemies.

Somewhere along their migratory trail southwestward from Minnesota to the Plains, the Cheyenne were joined by a small band known as the Suhtai. Black Kettle was a Suhtai, and it is believed that he was born near the Black Hills sometime around 1807. Little is known of his early life. Evidence indicates that he rode with war parties which came south during the 1820s to hunt and capture wild horses in Colorado. This group eventually split away from the northern group and took up residence on the Arkansas.

Like most Cheyenne males, Black Kettle was a warrior as a young man. Thus, he was undoubtedly involved in the many Cheyenne conflicts with the Pawnees, Utes, and other traditional enemies to the north. He may well have been involved, also, in Cheyenne forays against the Comanches of northern Texas and western Oklahoma. According to George Bent, who was married to Black Kettle's niece, Black Kettle was one of the Cheyenne scouts who discovered the Comanche-Kiowa camp preceding the 1838 Battle of Wolf Creek in northwestern Oklahoma.

The Cheyenne-Arapaho victory over the Comanches and Kiowas at Wolf Creek led to a great peace council with those tribes at Bent's Fort on the Arkansas River of present Colorado in 1840. There it was agreed among the tribes that the Cheyenne and Arapaho could range freely and in peace in the area south of the Arkansas that would eventually become their home.

In 1848 Black Kettle led an expedition against the Utes of the Rocky Mountain region. Though present, he was not yet a chief in 1851 when the United States conducted the Treaty of Fort Laramie, Wyoming, with most of the tribes in the region. By this pact the Cheyenne and Arapaho were assigned all the land between the Platte and Arkansas rivers from western Kansas to beyond the first range of the Colorado Rockies.

In 1853 Black Kettle was given the high honor of carrying the Cheyenne's Sacred Medicine Arrows into battle. It was soon after, following the death of Chief Old Bark (or Bear's Feather), that he was named a chief. As such, he was in command of his force of Cheyenne warriors when Colonel E. V. Sumner and his dragoons routed the Cheyennes with an unexpected saber attack on the Smoky Hill River in 1857.

Three years later, Black Kettle became a part of recorded U.S history as the lead signer of the Treaty of Fort Wise, along with White Antelope, Lean Bear, Little Wolf, and Tall Bear. Up to this time, Black Kettle and other Cheyenne leaders had had virtually no personal contact with white men. Certainly, they had no understanding of legal matters or the enormous value of their land and its minerals. Further, they were at the mercy of white interpreters who inserted their own interests into the treaty arrangements.

By the Treaty of Fort Wise, the United States took back all

of the land it had assigned the tribes under the Fort Laramie pact—land on which gold had been discovered—in exchange for a small, arid reservation in eastern Colorado. Little wonder, then, that when Black Kettle and the other chiefs realized how they had been duped, they repudiated the treaty.

The Colorado gold rush brought whites flooding across the Plains into what was then the home of the Southern Cheyenne and Arapaho. Though the Indians received the intruders with kindness and generosity, conflicts soon developed. These clashes were precipitated in most cases by lawless white men. They were further agitated by U.S. troops who conducted punitive strikes against the Indians.

One of the most blatant incidents involved a command of U.S. troops during the spring of 1864. This unit marched from Denver into western Kansas looking for Indians to attack. They eventually came onto a peaceful Cheyenne buffalo hunt headed by Chief Lean Bear. Only a year earlier, Lean Bear had visited with President Abraham Lincoln in the White House at Washington, D.C., and avowed his friendship.

The chief and another Cheyenne rode forward to show the troops Lean Bear's letter of recommendation from the President. It stated that he was a friendly Indian. Without warning or provocation, the troops shot both from their saddles and killed them.

This unwarranted murder of a much-loved chief drove the Cheyennes to war. Led by one of their war societies known as the Dog Soldiers, they ravaged Kansas transportation routes and frontier settlements during the summer of 1864.

Going against the war element of his tribe, Black Kettle sent word to Fort Lyon, Colorado, that he wished to make peace. Major Edward W. Wynkoop responded by leading a military expedition

Chief Black Kettle is seated at the center and White Antelope at the far left in this historic photograph of the Cheyenne-Arapaho delegation at Denver in 1864. Major Edward Wynkoop, in dark hat, kneels in front of Black Kettle.

to the headwaters of the Smoky Hill River. There he met in council with Cheyenne chiefs, who sat in a huge circle. Most of the faces were angry and hostile; but one, that of Black Kettle, stood out sharply to Wynkoop.

"He was one," the officer noted, "who had stamped on every lineament the fact that he was born to command."

The Cheyenne Principal Chief, Black Kettle, who had sat "calm, dignified, immovable with a slight smile," rose and embraced Wynkoop, leading him to the center of the circle. He then made a speech defying the Cheyenne war leaders and making clear his determination to make peace if possible.

In response to Wynkoop's demand for a return of white captives held by the tribe, Black Kettle used his own ponies to purchase the freedom of four white children. Then, even in the face of the recent murder of Lean Bear, he dared to lead a delegation to Denver to talk with territorial governor John Evans.

"We have come with our eyes shut," he told Evans, "following his [Wynkoop's] handful of men, like coming through the fire. The sky has been dark ever since the war began. All we ask is that we may have peace with the whites."

Evans showed little appreciation for Black Kettle's willingness to risk great danger in the cause of peace. Both he and Colonel John M. Chivington, a burly former minister who had risen to the post of military commander of Colorado Territory, were involved in hot political races. Both men had contributed to a panic situation among the white populace. People feared an Indian uprising similar to the Sioux outbreak that had occurred the previous year in Minnesota.

Evans accused the Indians of starting the war. He reiterated his instructions for all friendly Indians to go to military forts. He promised them military protection if they did so. This promise was reaffirmed by Chivington. Relying upon these assurances, Black Kettle returned to the prairie and led his band of Cheyennes in to Fort Lyon. He was told to camp on Sand Creek forty miles north of the fort where he would be safe from troops.

Despite this, and in direct violation of his promise, Chivington

*White Antelope, left, and other Cheyenne chiefs traveled to far-off Washington,
D.C., in 1851 to try to make peace with the white man.*

gathered the units under his command together and made a sunrise attack on Black Kettle's camp. He caught the sleeping Cheyenne village completely by surprise.

Chivington's assault drove the stunned Indians fleeing from the camp. The pursuing cavalry used cannon, saber, and pistol to strike down men, women, and children alike. Black Kettle and his wife managed to escape, though she received nine bullet wounds.

Chief White Antelope had visited Washington, D.C., following the Treaty of Fort Laramie and had accompanied Black Kettle to Denver. He was shot down at Sand Creek as he stood unarmed in the middle of the creek bed trying to halt the attack. His body was later mutilated by the troops.

Marked as it was by such blatant betrayal and "civilized" brutality, the Sand Creek Massacre became a symbol of white perfidy not only to the Cheyenne but to most tribes of the Central Plains. Even government officials and Americans in general realized the shame of Chivington's action.

Following the Sand Creek Massacre, the Cheyennes and Arapahos retreated to western Kansas. From there the Dog Soldiers and their allies conducted a war of revenge against the wagon routes along the Platte and Arkansas rivers, striking military stations and frontier settlements and cutting telegraph lines between.

In an effort to end their resistance, the government arranged for a new treaty at the mouth of the Little Arkansas, the site of present Wichita, Kansas. Famous frontiersmen Kit Carson and William Bent were called upon to help. Black Kettle, though he had been direly threatened by the Dog Soldiers, attended the meeting and signed a new peace agreement.

"My shame is as big as the earth," he told the peace commission. "I once thought that I was the only man that persevered to be the

The site of the Sand Creek Massacre is much the same today as it was in 1864 when Chivington's troops attacked the Cheyenne camp.

friend of the white man, but since they have come and cleaned out our lodges, horses, and everything else, it is hard for me to believe white men anymore."

None of the Cheyenne war chiefs signed the treaty, however, and the pact was doomed to failure. The implacable anger and hatred of the Dog Soldiers over white intrusion onto their hunting grounds had not diminished. They refused to follow Black Kettle's band south of the Arkansas.

Still another treaty council was conducted in 1867 on Medicine Lodge Creek in southern Kansas. The Kansas-Pacific Railroad was being built across western Kansas, and the government wished to remove the Dog Soldiers and other Indians. Black Kettle signed the treaty as the Second Chief behind Bull Bear, leader of the Dog Soldiers. This was indication of the power of the war societies among the Cheyenne at that time.

During the summer of 1868, rebellious young warriors raided white settlements along the Saline and Solomon rivers of central Kansas. These depredations incited the white citizens of Kansas to demand that the army punish the Indians. Major General Phil Sheridan had recently been placed in charge of the military district that included Kansas and the Indian Territory (now Oklahoma). He was ready and willing to go to war.

He laid plans for a winter campaign into the Indian Territory. By it he hoped to strike the Indians as they held to their villages during cold, snowy weather. The campaign would be a three-pronged strike. One command would march from Fort Bascom in New Mexico; another from Fort Lyon in Colorado; and a third, the main force led by the 7th Cavalry, from Fort Larned, Kansas.

Sheridan also issued instructions for peaceful Indians to go to Fort Cobb in the Indian Territory and turn themselves over to authorities there. Black Kettle attempted to do so. General William M. Hazen offered to accept him but not his band. Black Kettle refused to leave his people, even though Hazen warned him that Sheridan had troops in the field.

Returning to his camp on the Washita, Black Kettle met with his chiefs. They agreed that their location—the furthermost west of numerous Cheyenne, Arapaho, Kiowa, Comanche, and Plains Apache camps stretching along the river for several miles—was a dangerous one. Tomorrow they would move.

They did not know that Sheridan had already established Camp Supply not far to the north at the conflux of Beaver and Wolf creeks. Nor were they aware that Sheridan had ordered Custer and the 7th Cavalry to the field in search of Indians at their home camps, saying:

"Destroy their villages and ponies. Kill or hang all warriors, and bring back all women and children."

A heavy snowstorm was raging as Custer departed Camp Supply and moved southwestward from Wolf Creek. True to Custer's hopes, the snow-covered ground aided in finding tracks of an Indian war party west of the Antelope Hills. Though the tracks had been made by Kiowas, they led southward to the Washita River and Black Kettle's village.

Custer's force arrived at the site during the middle of the night. He deployed his troops to encircle the fifty-tipi village and waited for dawn to attack. The conflict began when a Cheyenne man emerged from his lodge to check on a barking camp dog. Spotting a soldier's head across the river, he fired a warning shot from his rifle. Custer immediately ordered his bugler to sound the charge.

Once again, just as it had been almost exactly four years earlier, Black Kettle's village was invaded by whooping, firing, saber-wielding cavalry troops. The defenders of the village were easily overwhelmed, and the fleeing occupants were chased down without mercy. As customary for chiefs, Black Kettle kept a horse by his tipi. He mounted the horse and with his wife behind, attempted to escape down the river. They were shot from the horse's back in mid-stream, and both killed.

Custer ordered the Cheyennes' lodges burned and all of their eight hundred captured ponies shot. He then retreated back to Camp Supply with fifty-three women, children, and babies. In his report to Sheridan and to newspapers around the nation, Custer reported that he had won a great victory.

Black Kettle had done all he could to make peace with the white man. But in the end, like Lean Bear and White Antelope, he was rewarded with death.

Today the Cheyenne people regard the massacres of Black Kettle's villages at Sand Creek and the Washita as the most signal events in their history. The two attacks have come to epitomize the injustices which the Cheyenne have suffered in their relations with white Americans.

These Cheyenne women and children, photographed at Camp Supply, were taken captive at the Washita.

"Cheyenne children," Chief Rollin Haag observed, "hear the story of Sand Creek and Washita over and over in their homes. It is a way to explain how we lost our land and freedom on the prairie.

"But Black Kettle's story is more than that. It can help others understand and appreciate how the Indian has always tried to live in harmony with white people. We think that a great man such as Black Kettle should be revered by all Americans."

3

The Sacred Arrow Tradition

IT IS LATE JUNE and the time of the summer solstice. The sun blazes at its zenith as the sounds and shapes and movements of past ages are reenacted on a grassy hilltop near the small town of Seiling in western Oklahoma. During the day, Indian men move about clearing the area, erecting tents and tipis, and building brush arbors. Women and girls are busy, also. They arrange their camps, dig pits for their cooking fires, and prepare meals.

Soon an encampment has taken form. The crosspoles of tipis strike against the sky, rimming the campsite. They give the land the ancient look of yesterday's frontier. In the surrounding countryside, wheat harvest is underway. Hungry combines gnaw their way around ripened fields. Trucks lumber back and forth to grain elevators until finally work is stymied by darkness.

Even as the weary harvest crews end their long day's work,

from the hill the throbbing beat of an Indian drum begins to pulsate in the cooling night air. The shapes of dancers oscillate in and out of the flickering camp lights. Two very different cultures brushed shoulders this day. Each is the result of long traditions, and each represents a distinct mode of life.

This Indian gathering is no public show; few non-Cheyennes even know of it. It is purely a tribal affair involving two annual traditions that speak to the very soul of the Southern Cheyenne Indians. They are the Sacred Medicine Arrow Renewal and the annual Sun Dance.

These rituals have been handed down among the Cheyenne from generation to generation since the time the tribe first began hunting buffalo during the late seventeenth century. Though long divided geographically, the Southern Cheyenne remain as one with the Northern Cheyenne of Montana in reverence for these tribal traditions. They hearken to the days when the Cheyenne were unified as a proud and independent nation.

The Sacred Medicine Arrow Renewal tradition, which is unique to the Cheyenne, has special meaning to them even today. Like other Indian tribes, they are a tribal family that is fighting to keep itself from being broken apart by the crush of American empire and the influences of a changing world.

"The Sacred Arrow Renewal is a prayer to the Heaven Spirit, Maheo," states headman and tribal representative George Sutton of Canton, Oklahoma, who recently participated in the ceremony. "We pray for peace and goodness for the Cheyennes, for all Indians, and for all of mankind. This is the Cheyenne New Year; everything is made new again."

These several days of ceremony and festivities involve the gathering of Southern Cheyennes from over Oklahoma and be-

George Sutton, a Cheyenne-Arapaho tribal representative, erects his own personal lodge for the Arrow Renewal and Sun Dance with the help of Sam American Horse, Moses Starr, and George's son Chauncey.

yond, as well as Northern Cheyennes from their Montana reservation. All year the Seiling ceremonial grounds have stood weeded and vacant except for a few stunted Chinese elms. During mid-June the site undergoes a transformation of people and activity.

First, members of the Cheyennes' Kit Fox, Bowstring, Elk, and Dog Soldier warrior societies come to mow the area. While this is being done, those involved in the Arrow Renewal set up their camps. More and more people arrive during the two weeks of ceremony. Their cars, pickups, and vans are loaded with camping gear, food, and presents. The vehicles will bear tags from New York to California, reflecting the migration of some tribal members.

Eventually the hilltop will be encircled by tents, brush arbors, and tipis. From atop a tall lodge pole, the U.S. flag is whipped about by the prairie wind. At the center of the compound stands the Sacred Medicine Arrow Tipi. It is presided over by a Cheyenne priest known as the Keeper of the Arrows. Nearby are two other ceremonial tipis: the Offering Tipi and the Lone Tipi or Big Tipi. Each plays a role in the Arrow Renewal and Sun Dance.

"To the Cheyennes," commented Willie Fletcher, "the event is even more than a religious ritual. It's an annual reunion of our tribal family, a chance to see distant relatives and old friends. Once a year we can celebrate being Cheyenne and Indian and forget the troubles we know as a people. We pray for good health and for a return of the good times we once knew when we were masters of our own fate."

Origin of the Sacred Medicine Arrows is embedded in Cheyenne tribal lore. Cheyenne tradition tells that Maheo created the world and the people and all the animals and birds of the earth. Some of these—the coyote, the buffalo, and the eagle in

Northern Cheyennes Steve Brady (right) and his sons, Steve Jr., Dana, and Luke, arrive at the Seiling, Oklahoma, ceremonial grounds with a load of lodgepole pines for the Arrow Renewal and Sun Dance ceremonies.

particular—have magical powers. The four sacred spirits of Maheo reside in the four cardinal directions from which the wind comes. Even today the ceremonial pipe is puffed to them in reverence.

According to Cheyenne oral history, the Medicine Arrows (Mahuts) were brought to the Cheyenne by a very wise man. He was Sweet Root Standing, who as a youth had left the tribe after an argument with a chief. He wandered alone on the prairie for four years. During this time all the buffalo and other animals disappeared, and there was great famine over the land.

When Sweet Root Standing returned, he had the Cheyennes arrange their tipis into a great circle. Their openings were to face the east from where the sun rises each day. Then he sang to Maheo for four days and four nights, calling the buffalo to come back. The buffalo and other game returned, and the people were very thankful.

"Because of your magical powers," they told the boy, "we will now call you Sweet Medicine."

Several years later, Sweet Medicine and his wife went into the Black Hills to a place called Medicine-pipe Mountain. There in a great cave they met the four sacred spirits of Maheo, which became known to the Cheyenne as the Listeners-under-the-Ground.

The spirits gave Sweet Medicine four magical arrows that were painted black and red and beautifully adorned with eagle feathers. Two were Buffalo Arrows. They would assure a plentiful supply of buffalo. The other two were Man Arrows. Their powers would help the Cheyenne win victory over their enemies.

"These are to aid your people in peace and war," the spirits told Sweet Medicine. "Take them and hold them close, always."

After four years Sweet Medicine returned with the Sacred Arrows wrapped in a coyote skin. He told the people:

"Carry these Sacred Arrows when you go to war. They will give you food to eat and make you safe in your lodges."

Sweet Medicine then taught them many things that he had learned from the Maheo spirits: how to kill buffalo, tan hides, and make robes. He also taught them not to kill one another and not to steal. Sweet Medicine was never a warrior; he was a prophet and a teacher. Most of all, he was a peacemaker.

As is to be expected with oral traditions, there have been variations in the conduct of the Arrow Renewal, as described by Cheyenne scholars through the years. It is customary to open the Arrow Renewal ceremony with a sunrise raising of the United States flag and a prayer. During the first day the camp crier, wearing his white sash of respect, positions himself at the center, facing east, and sings a song in the Cheyenne language, asking Maheo for guidance.

Each year one or more men who wish to make vows to Sweet Medicine take part in the ceremony as "pledgers" to the ritual. Dressed only in a sheet and their bodies covered with red pigment, they march in single file to the Offering Tipi, where a priest has been closeted. He has been "cooking the beads" to produce a blue teardrop object known as "Blue Sky," representing the universe. The pledgers stroke themselves with it as an act of purification.

They then go to the Lone Tipi, taking a bundle of sacred objects and other gifts. The Arrow Keeper in turn gives them two small red roots, which they rub on their faces to protect themselves against the great power of the Medicine Arrows. The men are blessed, and the medicine pipe is offered to Maheo.

During the second day, the Arrow Keeper sends the pledgers to bring the Medicine Arrow bundle from the Arrow Tipi to the Lone Tipi. Now sweet grass, representing the hair of Sweet Medicine, is burned over a glowing coal inside the Lone Tipi. The Arrow Keeper offers a prayer; then he prepares an altar of sand where he sand-paints an outline representing the "Land of the Cheyennes" as it was originally made by Maheo.

Meanwhile, a priest sets up two pairs of forked sticks, each with a cross stick. This rack, upon which the Arrows will be placed during the ceremony, represents the "Blood of the Cheyenne" or the Cheyennes themselves. The Arrow Keeper places four hot coals upon the corners of the altar with a long, wooden fire-spoon. He burns braids of sweet grass over the coals as offerings to Sweet Medicine, and the various steps of the ceremony are monitored with counting sticks.

On the third and last day, the Arrow Keeper opens the Medicine Bundle and carefully lays the Sacred Arrows out on a sage bed covered with a square of red offering cloth. After positioning them on the Cheyenne-blood sticks, the arrows, along with several sacred objects, are tied meticulously to a pole. Then, singing to Maheo as they walk and pausing to turn four times, the pledgers take the pole and coyote skin to a prepared spot outside the tipi.

The men and boys of the encampment now come to see the Arrows and pray to Maheo. None of the women, however, can even look in the direction of the exposed Arrows.

After a time, the Arrows are returned to the Lone Tipi. There they are exposed to a buffalo skull, representing the Sacred Buffalo Hat (Is'-si-wun), which was brought to the Cheyenne when they were joined by their Suhtai branch. The Arrow Keeper, with prayers, burning of more sweet grass, and singing of four sacred songs, returns the Arrows to their coyote-skin bundle.

White-robed Sun Dance priests are visible at left in this 1890 panoramic view of a Cheyenne village near Fort Reno.

The Sacred Buffalo Hat, now kept by the Northern Cheyenne, is made from the skin of a buffalo cow's head, with carved buffalo horns attached. It, too, has special powers in both peace and war. It was given to the Suhtais' cultural hero, Standing on the Ground, by Maheo. Maheo's four spirit helpers instructed Standing on the Ground about the Sacred Buffalo Hat and also taught him the Sun Dance.

When the ritual is finished, the participants will usually cleanse themselves of the power of the Arrows in a small, igloo-shaped sweat lodge, where steam is produced by pouring water over heated rocks.

The Sun Dance, which follows the Arrow Renewal, was once a warrior indoctrination rite. Today it is a highly spiritual event to the pledgers who, wearing only a waist garment and bedecked in body paint, dance out their vows around a central pole in the Sun Dance lodge to the beat of an Indian drum.

The dancers are attended by sponsors, who sit behind them. These men instruct and encourage the participants as well as repaint them for the various dances. During intermissions the dancers are given vocal support by Cheyenne women, whose chant is referred to as "lu-luing."

Renewal of the Sacred Medicine Arrows and the Sun Dance hold a deep and abiding place among the Southern Cheyenne and the teachings of Sweet Medicine remain their most precious sacrament.

▷ 4 ◁

Cheyennes in Today's World

CONTRARY TO the old stereotype of the stoic American Indian, the Cheyennes are an outgoing people with a strong and active sense of humor among themselves. Laughter comes easily for them. They recite stories, some true and some not; and they tell jokes, often about the white man. They are reluctant, however, to open up to outsiders whom they do not know well.

"Cheyennes," a well-educated Cheyenne woman noted, "are always conscious of being Cheyenne. Inwardly many of them are still outsiders to the white man's world and its way of thinking, just as the white man is to theirs."

The Cheyennes today dress much in the manner of whites and have come to enjoy many of the advantages of modern society. They appreciate the automobile, television, prepared foods, and other items. But they intensely desire not to be like the white people in other ways. They hold strongly to being "Indian" and "Cheyenne." It is the essence of their fierce pride; their greatest fear is the loss of their tribal identity.

There has been an alarming erosion of cultural being among some of their youth, but there is still a strong affection for and affiliation to "the old ways" in the hearts and souls of most Cheyennes. The old men find great comfort in thinking and talking about the old days and singing the old songs. Elders continue to teach the young that courage, generosity, and strength of character are important.

There are few Cheyennes who, having left home, will not soon return to visit, attend the tribe's annual Sacred Medicine Arrow Renewal and Sun Dance, or come to take part in a powwow or a dance. Deep inside them is an unstoppable love for the beat of the dance drum, the smell of a wood fire, the taste of Indian food, the familiar, smiling faces of their own kind—and a spiritual devotion to all that is Cheyenne.

The Indian's feeling about his place in modern America was reflected in a valedictory address of an Indian teen-ager.

"It is our right," he said, "to become educated and join in with white American society if we wish. But it is also our right to live as Indian people."

Before they lost the land to the white settler, the Cheyennes were their own masters on the Plains. Stories of their past glories have been passed down generation by generation. In spirit, their Cheyenne ancestors still ride the prairie, hunting the buffalo, moving their camps from stream to stream, and living the life that only the Plains Indian once knew but knows no more.

Many young Cheyennes today are becoming more and more interested in the material things of the modern world. They find

Joe Antelope, who has been a Southern Cheyenne chief for many years, is deeply saddened by the erosion of Cheyenne culture.

it economically unrewarding to practice the Cheyenne way of life, and this worries the older ones. Even for the elders, memories of the old days are becoming fainter and fainter with each passing year.

"When I was a boy," Chief Joe Antelope, who was born in

1906, mused sadly, "I never saw a buffalo. We hunted deer and turkey, but I never saw a buffalo. They were all gone."

Joe, a descendant of Chief White Antelope, who was at one time the Keeper of the Arrows, has been a member of the traditional Cheyenne council of forty-four chiefs for over twenty-five years and is also a priest in the Native American Church. He is one of the few members of his tribe who still knows some of the old Indian sign language.

"I used to know it pretty good," the kindly, soft-spoken old man said. "But then there was nobody to talk to, and I forgot some of the signs. The old ways are fading. Not very many people even speak Cheyenne much anymore."

When he became a chief, Joe was given the rules and regulations that went with the office. He was told that a chief was required to be a good person, to offer advice on the right side of life, and to teach young people to respect their elders.

Cheyennes such as Joe feel strongly that their value system of inner worth is far better than the white man's materialistic desire to own things. Many older women, the grandmothers, show their feelings in the way they dress. They do not want to look like white women. They want to look like Indians. Today, they prefer to wear a black shawl, dark dress, and carry a black handbag. Sunglasses have become a standard part of their attire.

Cheyennes remember more than just the good side of the past. They also remember well the wrongs that were done to them. The long history of injustices they suffered as a people has shaped their attitude toward whites and non-Indian culture in general.

This, in turn, has made Cheyenne parents suspicious of the white man's schools. It is still true that the tribal member, especially a young male, who goes away to school or joins the work regimen of the white man's world invites criticism at home. It is not impossible that his tribal friends will ridicule and make fun of him. They may accuse him of trying to become a white man—an "apple," red on the outside and white on the inside—or that he is "white-man educated."

The Cheyenne family does not function like the average non-Indian family. It is typical for a young couple to move into the home of the wife's parents where all share in whatever income there is. Cheyenne families never hesitate about sharing their homes, their food, and whatever wealth they may possess.

"Sharing has long been a key to our survival," a Cheyenne leader notes. "It is one of our greatest strengths today, just as it was in the old days. When a camp was attacked, survivors would flee to another village. There they would be taken into lodges of others and helped as long as was necessary. We still take care of one another."

Friends share with friends. Much is given to those in need. The "give-aways" at dances and other events is a central Cheyenne custom. Sharing one's wealth is so ingrained in Cheyenne culture that it, in fact, tends to be resistive to ambition. As one observer put it: the more you have, the more you have to share. It does little good, therefore, to try to accumulate goods and wealth in the manner of the white man.

Quite often the grandmother becomes the one who raises the children rather than the parents. This has become more prevalent in modern times because of the high divorce rate and unwed teenage mothers. Indian people suffer from many of the same social ills that affect the main population.

Cheyenne homes are mostly small two-bedroom, frame buildings, usually austere and in need of repair. Repairs are often not possible on the meager income of a Cheyenne household. Many Indian people who were raised in dire poverty were simply never taught how to care for a house. They may have grown up in a tipi or tent with side toilet and no running water and have never learned to tend to a building structure.

Some tribal members have been fortunate to secure brick homes under the U.S. Housing and Urban Development (HUD) program, though these houses, too, have limited space and are generally poorly built. HUD, which operates through the Cheyenne and Arapaho housing authority, has built some 270 homes in thirteen Cheyenne and Arapaho communities. These are modern two-and three-bedroom homes that tribal members can rent or mortgage for low monthly payments.

A former official, a Cheyenne who worked with the program for two years before resigning in disgust, claims that the builders skimped on materials, using poorest quality plywood, decking, and plumbing. Many tribal members are displeased at the rapid deterioration of their HUD homes.

Employment, too, is a serious problem for Oklahoma Indians. Even in good times, jobs in the small Oklahoma towns are severely limited. The unemployment rate for Cheyennes and Arapahos in Oklahoma is well above 60 percent.

"For the Indian man or woman," noted Tom Burns, who heads the tribal educational department, "there just isn't much work at home. There are a few jobs in stores and filling stations, and some seasonal employment can be found on farms during harvest time. But that's about it."

A scattering of small industries, such as the Hollytex Spinning Mill at Watonga, employ a few Indian people. Many Cheyennes do not hold regular jobs. As a result, they depend heavily upon financial support from various social services or tribal assistance programs.

Though their reservation has been dissolved, the Southern Cheyenne and Arapaho still have tribal-held land holdings from which they derive grazing, farming, and oil and gas revenue. This income, plus money garnered from smoke shop revenue and the proceeds of tribal-operated Bingo, is distributed annually on a per capita basis. For tribal members who depend upon it to live, the amount is pitifully small.

The smoke shops are a relatively new enterprise that became available when Indian tribes proved in court that tribal sovereignty was a treaty right established with the federal government. This set them apart from the state governments and gave them exemption from tobacco tax. Thus, they can sell tobacco products at lower prices than state-regulated businesses, though this is under legal challenge. The tribes can also operate Bingo parlors in Oklahoma. Tobacco sales and Bingo games have become lucrative enterprises for a number of Indian tribes, including the Cheyenne and Arapaho.

Food items are issued monthly to households that fall below the poverty line through the U.S. Department of Agriculture's commodity program. The program is monitored by the Cheyenne and Arapaho Social Services office at the Concho headquarters. Tribal members can receive their commodities at the food distribution center at Weatherford, Oklahoma, or, by filling out an item request form in advance, at specified hometown sites by truck.

Because of the large distribution area, many pick up their requested goods from the truck "tailgate" deliveries. In addition to canned meats, juices, fruits, and vegetables, the program participants are provided a variety of items such as beans, rice, corn-

Reba Rednose receives her monthly commodities from a tribal tailgate delivery at Kingfisher, Oklahoma.

meal, flour, cheese, butter, canned and dried milk. Those eligible but not on the commodity program can opt for food stamps.

Older Cheyennes tell of their sparse childhood days before food distribution began. The late Bobby Big Horse recalled that he had never tasted milk until the day when someone brought a bottle to his home.

"I remember taking a sip of that strange, white stuff," Bobby said with a grin, "then spitting it out on the ground in disgust."

Many Cheyennes suffer from diabetes, and some think this is related to the effects of their eating the white man's regimen in place of the old-time Indian diet, which consisted heavily of meat, berries, and roots.

The Cheyennes and Arapahos are provided health care benefits by the federal government as a treaty right. The U.S. Public Health Service operates Cheyenne and Arapaho health centers at Watonga, Clinton, and Concho. A survey indicated that the major disabilities suffered by tribal members are hypertension, diabetes, heart disease, and alcoholism.

Like all Indians, the Cheyennes love and enjoy sports. The high schools of western Oklahoma have seen many outstanding Cheyenne athletes in both boys' and girls' sports. Cheyenne parents take great pride in the athletic endeavors of their children. Long after their own playing days are over, a Cheyenne father or mother will drive miles to see their son or daughter perform.

In addition to school-sponsored events, the Indian sports league known as UNITY offers competition for children of all Oklahoma tribes in football, baseball, basketball, softball, and track. Girls participate in the latter three sports.

Five Oklahoma Indian high schools, sponsored by the Bureau of Indian Affairs, are involved in this sports league. They are Sequoyah at Tahlequah, Jones Academy at Hartshorne, Carter Seminary at Ardmore, Riverside at Anadarko, and the Indian school at Eufaula. Winning teams and participants receive trophies, along with trips and other awards.

While many of the graduating Indian athletes are offered athletic scholarships at colleges and universities, not many of them accept. Disappointed tribal leaders blame the discomfort of Indian children among white society. Some state institutions of higher education, however, have implemented programs to make the Indian student feel more comfortable on their campuses.

Despite the ebbing away of their language and traditions and disaffection of the young from many of the traditional ways, the Southern Cheyennes still maintain their culture through commemorative ceremonies, benefit memorials, clan meetings, powwows, dances, and other events.

The dance is a significant element of Cheyenne culture. It is by far the most popular form of entertainment and socializing for the Cheyennes. An Indian social dance, however, is much different from the personal, romantic dance of white society. It is a tribal communal affair in which the entire family from grandparent to grandchild participates. Many elders come not, perhaps, to take part in the dance, but simply to watch and enjoy the performance of the dancers.

A dance is generally held inside an unpretentious metal building or, in hot weather, outdoors. Having brought their own chairs, the people seat themselves with Indian patience around the walls of the otherwise empty structure until the food tables have been set up. After a prayer has been said to bless the gathering and when the people all have eaten, time has come for the festivities to begin. Normally the U.S. colors are presented by an Indian honor guard of war veterans.

Dances are often sponsored by individual families, a tribal society, or an organization. Sometimes it will be a benefit dance for someone who has a special hardship or misfortune or to honor a serviceman, a graduate, or someone's birthday. It may also be held to commemorate a historical happening or to raise funds for a forthcoming event or worthy cause.

Often dances are held for members of all Indian tribes who

Above: A Cheyenne gourd dance was held in honor of Minnie Red Hat, widow of former Arrow Keeper Ed Red Hat.

Left: Augustine Red Hat of Canton serves food at ceremonies preceding the dance honoring her grandmother.

wish to participate. If a dance involves a contest, there may be a grand entrance of dancers in fancy costumes of brilliantly colored feathers, cloths, and bells. Many Indian dancers make the dance circuit of various tribes to vie for prizes and win recognition. Funds for prizes may have been raised by benefit dances, bake sales, or Indian taco dinners.

The program for a dance is opened by an emcee, who makes his announcements. Then the head drummer begins pounding out a beat on the drum and singing a Cheyenne song. He is joined by other drummers—some with their long, black hair tied in braids or ponytails, others wearing weather-beaten cowboy hats or old visor caps that promote products—who seat themselves around the drum to take up the beat and the song.

Dancing is a spiritual experience for the performers, and the dance circle has special meaning in signifying the unity of the Cheyenne people and the whole of the universe. For virtually everyone except mere babies and the very old, dancing is a favorite form of entertainment. It truly is in their tribal blood.

Indeed, the benefit dance is more than entertainment. It is often a medium for generous gift-giving. In addition to the covered dishes of food for the meal, people bring clothes baskets loaded with "give-away" goods. This uniquely Indian form of gift-giving normally consists of utilitarian items such as blankets, clothing, and canned food but sometimes, also, money.

After the dance, these gifts are presented to the honoree, who uses them to reward those taking part in the dance, keeping only what is left. Thus, through the dance, the young are taught the qualities of community-sharing and generosity that are deeply ingrained in the Cheyenne character.

Cheyenne tribal members belong to various religious denom-

Calvin Old Camp, who is studying to become a respiratory therapist, is dressed for a traditional Cheyenne dance.

inations, since many churches have had missionaries working among the Oklahoma tribes for many years. More than a few Cheyennes are included in the estimated 100,000 Indian members of the Native American Church. The church, which promotes Christian teaching, has no formal meeting buildings.

The Native American Church is presently involved in a court challenge over its use of the drug, peyote. Use of the small hallucinogenic cactus pod was introduced among Oklahoma tribes during the 1890s by a Paiute Indian religious prophet, Wovoka, from Arizona. Native American Church members see attempts to restrict their practice of ingesting small amounts of peyote during their religious rites as an infringement on their religious freedom.

Wovoka prophesied the coming of an Indian-oriented Christ, the expulsion of whites from the Indians' land, and the return of the buffalo and other animals. The severely oppressed Oklahoma Indians were in a highly receptive condition for these preachings. Such great hope was aroused among the Cheyennes that they placed an iron bed atop Coyote Hill near Geary, Oklahoma, for use by the new savior.

The Cheyennes are strongly devoted to their spiritual beliefs that have sustained them through difficult times. Throughout their Sacred Medicine Arrow Renewal and in all of their ceremonies, Maheo and Sweet Medicine are honored. The four sacred spirits of Sweet Medicine are also recognized in these rites by repetitive homage to the four cardinal directions.

The Cheyennes' past remains a strong part of their present.

▷ 5 ◁

A Love for Mother Earth

THE CHEYENNE homeland in western Oklahoma today has the look and feel of the Plains Indian stronghold it once was. It is a land of rolling countryside and wide horizons. Though essentially prairie, extensive areas are still spotted with juniper, mesquite, sagebrush, and shinnery oak. Flat-topped buttes, created by prehistoric erosions, stand as silent witnesses to the march of time and the evolution of mammal and man.

Along the rivers here Cheyenne villagers once found berries and edible roots, bois d'arc trees that provided wood for bows, dogwood for arrow shafts, and flint for arrow points. Roaming buffalo herds provided meat and suet to eat, hides for lodges, robes for beds, sinews for bowstrings, and leather for ropes, halters, and many other uses. The needs of Cheyenne families were further attended through the winter months by an abundance of deer, rabbits, and other small game.

Today western Oklahoma is wheat and cattle country. The farmer and the cattleman are in possession of the majority of the land. They are the descendants of a generation of early settlers who arrived with fervent hopes of finding their share of the American dream. Americans had scurried across the continent to California in 1849 and to Colorado in 1859 in search of gold. Then, during the last decade of the nineteenth century, they rushed to the new Oklahoma Territory—as the western half of the Indian Territory had become known—to obtain land.

Few were much concerned that this country had been promised to the Indian "for so long as the grass grows and the waters flow." The farmer had his own survival to worry about. To him, ownership of land meant the opportunity to work and to secure the wondrous blessings of a bountiful America. If taking the Indians' home was a moral crime, it was the government official who had committed it, not the settler. The guilt—if it was accepted as that—seldom made its way back to the masses.

This is cattle country, also. Even before the settlers came, Texas cattlemen drove their great herds of longhorn cattle across here to Kansas railheads at Abilene, Wichita, and Dodge City. Some rested their herds along the way, fattening them on the rich grasslands of the Indian Territory before taking them on to market. Eventually, the cattlemen began leasing vast acres of the Indian reservations, establishing permanent operations. It was these ranchers who first broke the pristine openness of the prairie with their rupturing strands of barbed wire.

The cattleman and cowboy brought with them the vestiges of a cow-country culture that have never completely faded away from western Oklahoma. With his six-gun, broad-brimmed hat, high-heeled boot, and jingling spur, the cowboy became the horseback hero of Wild West show, rodeo, and Western movie and fiction. He soon took the place of James Fenimore Cooper's noble warrior as a romantic figure in the imagination of the American public.

The Anglo-Saxon cowboy was, after all, much easier for most Americans to identify with than the troublesome tribesman who so fiercely resisted U.S. territorial expansion during the last half of the nineteenth century.

Neither was the exotic image of the cowboy lost on the farmer. He enhanced his own self-concept by adopting much of the cow-country dress and culture. Overalls and flat-heeled work shoes could never match the glamor of cowboy hats and boots. The modern-day pickup truck with gun rack in the rear window is a symbolic substitute for the cow pony and six-gun on the hip.

The farmer's straw hat has been reshaped to resemble that of the cowboy. The cowboy boot has been modified with a low heel to accommodate walking rather than horseback riding, but it still has the sharp-toed Western look. Many Indian men, as well, show a liking for the Western-cowboy motif.

Though the country of western Oklahoma is much the same as it was before the whites came, it bears the changes of modern America. Paved highways stretch from town to town, the principal artery being the east-west Interstate 40. The expressway parallels old Highway 66, route of the Dust Bowl exodus to California during the thirties. Down these modern pathways, electricity and telephone lines converge to where a distant water tower of a small community breaks the long, flat horizon. In the fields, oil pumps bob up and down like thirsty pelicans.

Today, the farmer and cattleman reign as stewards of the land. But they, too, are discovering that inevitably time brings change.

Above: Asphalt highways interconnect grain elevators which now tower above the former Cheyenne-Arapaho reservation in western Oklahoma.

Right: Bobbing oil pumps dot the pastures and wheat fields of a land where great buffalo herds once grazed.

Many of the small farm-trade towns that spot the region have been caught up in an evolving world. Once busy stores stand spent and ragged, their plate-glass windows staring empty-eyed along sparsely occupied main streets.

Twin stretches of rail across the prairie, now weed-infested and rusting, give evidence of the demise of the American railroad era. Some local lines have been kept active for transporting wheat from the giant grain elevators that tower here and there above the prairie. But other lines have been abandoned, and one day their iron tracks will be as forgotten and as unnoticed, perhaps, as the Indian, cattle, or military trails that in earlier days crossed this land and now lie hidden beneath the dust of passing time.

*Rusting tracks mark the demise of the railroads as routes of the early West,
along with Indian trails and wagon roads.*

Today Western men gather in the small town cafes for morning coffee. They discuss their plight and offer opinions on the condition of the world. On occasion they hold conversational postmortems for a farming friend who suffered a bankruptcy—or, perhaps, for one of those increasing number whose overwhelming debts have led to suicide.

These men remember the dust storms, the droughts, the grasshopper plagues, and the stock-killing blizzards. Neither farmers nor ranchers in western Oklahoma have ever known life to be easy or certain. Still, they somehow are bound to this hard country all the more for its testing of their metal.

Not unexpectedly, as with their forebears, their views of the destiny of this land are restricted largely to their own concerns. In truth, the white residents of western Oklahoma have given little sympathetic consideration to the welfare of their Indian neighbors.

In earlier times, the prejudice of whites against the resident Indians sometimes led to open hostilities. In 1903, old Chief Powder Face went to the aid of a tribesman who could not get a white man to stop cutting ice in a creek on his property. When the white man asked for help from the local sheriff, a deputy and five other men went out and shot Powder Face dead. The Cheyenne warriors rose up 160-strong and threatened to wipe out the small town of Taloga, Oklahoma. They were eventually pacified by the return of Powder Face's body.

The opportunistic white man flooded into Oklahoma during the first great land rush of 1889 and ensuing settlements of Indian reservations. To him the Indian appeared as lazy and unwilling to work for his share of society's benefits. The toiling granger was anxious to build homes and towns and create "a brand-new state" (as the song "Oklahoma" proclaims). He could little appreciate that the Indian simply was not driven by the same materialistic dreams of wealth.

Even today the Indian is largely an anachronism to most white citizens—an intrusive holdover from an age long gone by. Few have ever fully realized what injustices have been done the Indian in their behalf—that the United States had by force and connivance taken the land from the Indian and given it to them.

The Indian view, of course, is quite different. A proud, defiant people, the Cheyennes once fought wars with other Indian tribes for their right to live and hunt on the Central Plains. When the white man first came, they welcomed him with generous hospitality, accepted his treaty proposals, and attempted to accommodate a coexistence with him. The Indian was soon to find that cohabitation inevitably meant loss of land and way of life—the two things most crucial to him.

Seldom do non-Indians see the land and the role they and others play in the broader context of the ages as does the Indian. The mortality of man is expressed in a Cheyenne song that muses philosophically: "Nothing lives long, but the earth and the mountains."

The Cheyenne have always loved and respected that which once provided them all substance, their "Mother Earth." But their feeling for the land goes beyond ordinary emotion. To them it is an extension of Maheo, the All Father or the Wise One Above. The earth is an intimate part of their spiritual life. It lives. It nourishes. From it all things come. Man, before and after life, is but the earth's dust. Thus, it embodies the souls of their beloved ancestors.

The land cannot provide for them as it once did. The day of a hunter's existence is gone. Few Cheyennes have adapted either to farming or ranching. Today the tribe must look to lease income from their remaining lands, oil royalties, and the entrepreneurship of their smoke shops and Bingo parlors. It is not enough, and some members feel strongly that often these revenues do not filter down fairly to the people at large. It remains apparent that, while in the future more of their young will go out into the world and

Empty store fronts in towns such as Custer City are telltale to the changing fortune of the family farming community.

independently support themselves, the main tribal body is in dire need of financial assistance.

Some Indian leaders feel that the government is still failing to provide economic leadership that will help make the Indian self-sufficient.

"The government has no Indian economic program," noted a speaker at an American Indian symposium. "Indian people are supposed to remain welfare participants."

That the land no longer offers them sustenance has little effect upon the Cheyennes' love for it. Reverence for their Mother Earth in western Oklahoma as the spiritual sanctum of their forefathers remains an essential part of their cultural tradition. Moreover, their attachment to the earth provides the Cheyennes with a psychological foundation from which to face the challenges of an ever-threatening world.

6

In Social Exclusion

THE CHEYENNE-ARAPAHO reservation was opened to settlement by the general public on April 19, 1892, in a chaotic mass "land run" invasion. At a given signal, some 25,000 Americans made a wild dash for 160-acre homesteads from the 3.5 million acres of the reservation left after the Cheyennes and Arapahos had been forced to take individual allotments. This was another severe cultural shock to a people who had already endured much.

The taking of the reservation lands and the breaking up of the bands may have been progress to government officials, but to the Cheyenne people it was a deadly blow. For all of their known history, the Cheyennes had existed as tribal people, living in family bands closely associated with one another. Their entire being was as a member of the tribal unit.

From childhood they had been conditioned to rely upon the

interrelationship of the band and upon their chiefs and elders for support and help in the conduct of their lives. To be thus separated from the tribal family was much the same as a child being disassociated from its parents, siblings, and friends.

Still another factor intensified this separation and suffocation of culture. The Indians no sooner arrived at their new homes than they were surrounded by predominantly white neighbors. During one day's time, they became a one-to-ten minority on the land where they had been the sole occupants. As a result, many of them forsook their allotments and returned to their old camps.

Often white settlers, hoping to grab the Indian's allotment, did all they could to encourage his departure. They stole fence posts and wire, burned tipis and shot into them, pastured cattle on Indian allotments, and assaulted Indian women. They took the Indians' stock, claiming them to be strays and holding them for redemption. Indian property was often appropriated under pretext, knowing that the Indian owner was probably totally ignorant of his rights under the law.

The settlers complained bitterly that the Cheyennes and Arapahos had taken the best farming land. The Dawes Act of 1887 had originally provided protection against the Indian losing his land to whites with an "alienation" clause. The clause had established a twenty-five-year trust period for Indian land. However, in 1891 Congress made it possible for non-Indians to lease Indian land for a three-year period. Under this provision, whites were able to bilk Indian landowners with sharp deals.

By the turn of the century, the Cheyennes still faced enormous difficulty. Most lived in tipis in near-starvation conditions. Few cultivated land or were committed to any kind of industry, most leading lives of dissipation with gambling and heavy drinking.

In 1895 Cheyenne agent A. E. Woodson escorted this delegation of Cheyenne chiefs to Washington, D.C. They include (seated left to right) Little Wolf, Whirlwind, Little Chief, Cloud Chief, and White Horse.

The tribe continued to be cheated badly at every opportunity by traders and merchants—men who looked to the issuance of treaty payments with avaricious eagerness.

Agent A. E. Woodson praised those who courageously defied the tribal norms and made serious efforts at farming and raising cattle. One of these was Standing Bird, a former Cheyenne scout and policeman who planted and raised good crops of potatoes, corn, and cotton in Custer County.

Another was Chief White Antelope, a descendant of the White Antelope killed at Sand Creek. Despite his many years and infirmities, this good-hearted man worked his farm and, with his wife, kept a good home. Still, less than 20 percent of the Southern

Cheyenne were committed to agriculture by the turn of the century.

Cheyenne historian Don Berthrong notes in *The Cheyenne and Arapaho Ordeal*:

> Every aspect of Cheyenne culture was under stress, and the old ways of life were changing; the Indian could no longer dress as he wanted or wear his hair as had the old warriors; Indian marriages were illegal . . . Indians had to live among increasing numbers of white men and women; and all had to conform to the law of the white man.

These Cheyenne scouts, seen at the Darlington Agency in 1890, served with the U.S. Army during Oklahoma Territorial days.

The Burke Act of 1906 and further acts of Congress removed protection provided by the Dawes Act against whites obtaining Indian allotments. It became more and more possible for Indians to divest themselves of their land. Destitute allotment owners were often much too ready to sell their land for immediate reward, only to end up without home or food.

In 1909, two years after Oklahoma statehood, Dog Soldier Chief Mower pleaded with officials to restrict such sales: ". . . we don't know how to use our money," he said, "and speculators take money from us . . . They are standing ready to grab our land and money the moment it is in our possession."

Wolf Chief also insisted that his people needed government help in protecting them from themselves and white opportunists. "I am kind of afraid to take the white man's ways yet," he told a commissioner. "I don't know how to write. I don't know how to manage my affairs the white man's way."

The federal government was slow to hear and slower to act, however. As a result, there began a wholesale transfer of Cheyenne and Arapaho allotments to white hands, often as a result of white land sharks and schemers. More and more tribespeople found themselves with no tribal home, no reservation agency, no money, and no land.

Little has changed with the Southern Cheyennes through the ensuing years. Their social and economic exclusion, the erosion of their culture, the victimization of them by whites, and their own incompatibility with mainstream America have not gone away.

While some Cheyennes have found a place outside the tribal world, the majority of them continue to be excluded from the main course of American society. They remain embedded in a morass of social, economic, and personal difficulty. Many problems that young Cheyennes face today are related to lack of formal education.

School Indian counselor Quentin Roman Nose is dedicated to helping Indian children just as he himself was helped as a boy.

The high school dropout rate is of great concern to men such as Quentin Roman Nose. Quentin is a great-grandson of Henry Roman Nose for whom Roman Nose State Park was named and a descendant of Cheyenne Chief Sand Hill, who was killed at the Washita. He is also a college graduate with a B.A. in mathematics and a former U.S. Army officer.

Serious-minded and determined, Quentin is one of those who

made it through the Oklahoma school system despite its disfavor to Indian students.

"Of the twelve Indians in my first-grade class," he recalls, "I was the only one to graduate from high school."

He is especially concerned that most public schools offer very little, if any, education or information on Indian history. He feels that because the schools still hold to an overwhelming emphasis on white history, both in a regional and national sense, Indian youngsters learn nothing about their own race or tribe. They have no chance to read about significant Indian leaders, of which there were many, and thereby have no role models of their own kind.

"This is critical," Quentin notes. "It is difficult for a young Indian to identify with the heroes of American history as a non-Indian does. The inattention to Indian role models makes it hard for Indian students to develop a strong self-concept. This exclusion of the Native American in history books is abetted by a strong undercurrent of prejudice against him among whites in current times."

The Cheyennes want a more honest retelling of their history.

"The white man conquered the Indian," comments Nathan Hart, a Cheyenne and Director of the Oklahoma Indian Affairs Commission. "He also conquered the history. The records of Indian relations, the fighting, the manipulated treaties—they were all made by white men. Then other white men took these one-sided records and wrote history books. A lot of the time the Indian's truth has been shot out of the saddle. In fact, you might say it's been scalped.

"We need to get our young people interested in our culture and history and make them want to preserve it."

There has been some small movement in the Oklahoma public

schools to acquaint non-Indian children with Indian culture. On occasion, schools in Oklahoma City have invited Cheyenne Sun Dance priest, Willie Fletcher, to visit and tell about Cheyenne ways and what it's like to be Indian. Willie was also a great help to ethnologist Dr. John Moore of the University of Oklahoma in writing a book on Cheyenne demographics.

Frank Bushyhead, who holds a B.A. and two M.A. degrees and has taught classes in Indian education at Oklahoma City University, fully agrees. He feels that the Indian has been far too acquiescent in the face of white prejudice.

"I am teaching my children not to let whites intimidate them," he said. "When they run into bigotry, I want them to stand up and look people in the eye and calmly confront it."

Bushyhead, who manages health education for the Cheyenne and Arapaho tribes, is a talented artist and craftsman who produces a large variety of Cheyenne artifacts. He believes that much of white bias stems from a lack of understanding of Indian culture.

His mother, Ruby Bushyhead, who also works for the tribal government, is a firm believer in education attainment for Indian people. She feels that it is vital for them if they are to win equal status with whites.

Sherman Goose, a grandson of Wolf Chief, is another Cheyenne who holds great concern for his people and has strong ideas as to their condition. A pleasant face and friendly smile reflect his easygoing nature. But when this veteran infantryman of World War II and the Normandy invasion discusses the problems of the Southern Cheyenne, he becomes dead serious. He speaks his mind clearly and emphatically regarding bias against Indian youngsters in school.

"Education is very important to Indian children," Sherman

Cheyenne Sherman Goose of Arapaho, Oklahoma, served with the U.S. Army in Germany during and after World War II.

insists. "That's why prejudice in the school is so bad. It damages their self-pride and makes them want to drop out. Often it keeps Indian people from sending their children to school."

Sherman holds a deep, lingering anger at the discrimination that he has seen exercised against his race all his life. He has witnessed it in the school, the workplace, and even in the church. As one who believes strongly in education for Indian children, he is especially incensed at the racism expressed by many white classmates and sometimes by teachers against Indian students.

"I blame the parents of white children mostly," he says with a sad shake of his head. "They teach their children prejudice at home. For teachers, it's inexcusable."

The Johnson-O'Malley Act of the 1930s established a federal program of financial assistance for Indian children. These funds are allocated through the state to schools, principally to provide funds for textbooks, school supplies, and some extracurricular activities such as band and sports.

Some individuals, however, charge that the program has been badly misused by school superintendents and principals, that much of the money has been used to the benefit of non-Indian students. Dorothy Goodblanket, a strong-minded Cheyenne from Clinton who was a coordinator for the program in thirty-six schools of the Cheyenne and Arapaho reservation area, has been a thorn in the side of such school administrators on the matter. She knows of instances in which non-Indian parents, encouraged by a school principal, signed forms claiming Indian blood for their children so that they would benefit from the funds.

"One school principal," Dorothy claims, "sent out nearly two hundred forms to parents. He instructed them to sign the form if they suspected they had any Indian blood anywhere in their ancestry. There were only nine students who were actually qualified. Few Indian parents even knew of the program."

When Dorothy challenged the principal on the issue, she was ordered to stay away from the school. Other white administrators refused even to talk to her.

White prejudice is a particularly difficult problem for the Indians in Oklahoma. They have not forgotten that this land was originally designated as the "home of the Indian." When the Cheyennes were given citizenship by the government, they were no longer restrained by military troops from going where they pleased. However, they still remain subjected to the status of second-class citizenship in their home communities and elsewhere.

Older Cheyennes recall the day when they could not eat in Oklahoma cafes—and the sign in the store window of a small town that read: "No dogs or Indians allowed."

Bobby Big Horse, former state political lobbyist for Indian affairs, felt that Indians almost always got the lowest-paying jobs. He echoed the charge of prejudice, remembering with pain the time when he was rejected by the Boy Scouts, supposedly because the troop was already full. Though this particular situation has now changed, he felt deeply the psychic whip marks of the prejudice that he endured in school and experienced at different points in his life.

Terry Wilson is a Cheyenne Sun Dance priest with much experience in both the Sun Dance and Medicine Arrow Renewal ceremonies. A veteran of the Vietnam War, Terry attended Southwestern University at Weatherford, Oklahoma, where he majored in psychology and physical education.

Like many Indian veterans, he was unable to find a job when he returned home. As with other tribes, alcoholism is a serious problem for the Cheyennes. Like many of his friends, Terry began drinking heavily to the point of becoming an alcoholic. But then he secured a job with the Cheyenne & Arapaho Alcohol Treatment Center and gained control of his addiction.

A state-funded community action program in Watonga, which offers counseling and a thirty-day residential treatment program, holds weekly meetings. Modeled upon the successful Alcoholics Anonymous program, its fees are based entirely on the ability of its members to pay. Many of the program participants are Indian. Some attend under court orders because of law infractions, but others attend on their own. Another alternative is the halfway house at the Concho Cheyenne-Arapaho headquarters.

Though they have not forgotten the bitter betrayals of the past and live even yet under the stigma of white discrimination, the Cheyennes are proud, loyal Americans. The warrior tradition of the American Indian has been translated into meritorious service in the wars of the United States. The Cheyenne are by no means an exception; their young men have fought with great honor in all of the United States' wars of the twentieth century.

Harold Barse, director of the Oklahoma Vietnam Veterans Outreach Center, notes that during the Vietnam War 80 percent of Indian servicemen were volunteers. Most of them served in combat units, reflecting a very high casualty rate.

"It was almost certain," one Indian veteran commented with a wry laugh, "that if you were Indian, you walked point on patrol. You might say that we Indians were so stereotyped as scouts that we were too 'qualified' for our own good."

Barse observes that Plains Indian tribes still place a high value on warriorship. The returning veteran is always treated with a great deal of respect and honor.

"It is still the case," agrees Dolores Subia Big Foot-Sipes, who holds her Ph.D. in counseling psychology from the University of Oklahoma, "that many young Indian males can find greater recognition among their people through military service than by civil accomplishment."

Larry Roman Nose, Quentin's cousin, recounted a story of a Cheyenne elder who talked to a group of Indian boys preparing to go away to Germany to fight during World War II. Raymond Stone Calf, descendant of Chief Stone Calf, conducted prayers and ceremonies with them in a tipi.

"You are Cheyennes," he told them. "You have a rich heritage, and you should be proud to fight for the U.S. flag."

Cheyenne. 15.

Southern Cheyenne Chief Stone Calf and his wife were photographed during a visit to Washington, D.C. in 1873.

He showed them a United States flag and then described how the Cheyennes had captured such a banner when they helped the Sioux defeat General Custer at the Battle of the Little Bighorn.

"Your ancestors captured this flag," the Cheyenne elder said. "They took it back to their camp and displayed it. When you go to war, fight proudly for this flag. It belongs to you."

Larry, who served in Vietnam, described how during that conflict tribal leaders went to their sacred mountain at Bear Butte, South Dakota, to fast and pray for the war to end. When the war was over, the elders would sometimes place returning servicemen in sweat lodges to cleanse away any bad spirits that had been pushed up by the war.

Upon returning to civilian life, Indian veterans often find it hard to readjust. Their limited formal education plus the prejudiced job market makes it very difficult for them to earn a livable wage. Some work at odd jobs on a seasonal or on a temporary basis around their home communities.

The lack of small town employment has caused many young people to migrate to urban centers such as Oklahoma City, only to find the situation for them there is as bad or worse. Now outside the help of the tribal government, they find themselves without enough education, without job skills, and with no home or base support system. Often they become alcoholic street people. There they add to America's legacy of failure in dealing with victims of the nation's march of empire.

▷ 7 ◁

To Honor the Past

THE INDIAN TERRITORY —Oklahoma—was once seen by the federal government as the repository for many of the displaced Indian tribes of the nation. Today there are some thirty-six offices representing tribal governments within the state. Though the reservations have long since been terminated, the Indian heritage of the state is pronounced and deep-rooted.

By and large, non-Indian Oklahomans are truly proud of their state's Indian background. Much recognition has justly been given to Sequoyah, inventor of the Cherokee alphabet; to Jim Thorpe, the state's great Sac and Fox Olympic athlete; to the famous humorist Will Rogers, who possessed Cherokee blood; and to Indians in general. The likenesses of these men adorn the State Capitol, and their names have been applied to government buildings, public schools, state roads, and elsewhere.

Five world-famous Oklahoma ballerinas, all of Indian descent,

It was a Southern Cheyenne, Chief Wolf Robe, whose profile graced one side of the famous "buffalo nickel" in circulation in the 1930s.

were recently immortalized with a mural in the Oklahoma State Capitol. Entitled *Flight of Spirit*, it features the likenesses of Yvonne Chouteau, Cherokee; Rosella Hightower, Choctaw; Moscelyne Larken, Shawnee-Peoria; Maria Tallchief, Osage; and Marjorie Tallchief, Osage. The mural artist was Mike Larsen, a member of the Chickasaw tribe. Dedication of the mural on November 17, 1991, marked Oklahoma's celebration of "The Year of the Indian."

But, uniquely, such attention has generally failed to translate into public sympathy for the plight of impoverished tribespeople. Unquestionably, cultural and economic differences contribute greatly to this. But many Indians charge that the state has not effectively incorporated an appreciation for their culture and their great men into its public school curriculum.

"I was amazed," tribesman Walter Hamilton commented, "to discover that my oldest son, a high school graduate, did not know who Jim Thorpe was. But that's how little is taught about the Indian people in Oklahoma schools."

Oklahoma Indians feel, also, that their image has been badly misused for commercial purposes in advertising billboards and tourism promotional pieces by those who evidence little real-life concern for Indian people. The truth of this charge is inescapable. However, in recent times there have been some improvements. This has been achieved in part by drawing attention to other great Indians of their past, such as Black Kettle.

The tribes are also making their unique and colorful cultures more and more visible to the non-Indian public. An outstanding effort toward this end is the Red Earth Festival held in Oklahoma City each June. Existence of the festival owes much to Oklahoma Supreme Court Justice Yvonne Kauger, who was raised near the old Cheyenne community of Colony, Oklahoma. The Cheyenne

Labor Day powwow at Colony is said to be the oldest in the state.

As a child, Justice Kauger was personally acquainted with many of the Cheyenne chiefs of the past.

"It is really tragic," she observes, "that we let these living legends die away without making oral histories of their lives—and that they were not made available to Oklahoma school children."

Her strong interest in Cheyenne heritage caused Justice Kauger to found the Gallery of the Plains Indian at Colony. It has led in turn to the Red Earth Festival, which is dedicated to the preservation and development of Indian culture through various art forms.

During the annual Red Earth Festival of 1989, a large statue of an Indian woman was placed in front of the Oklahoma Capitol building as a symbol of the Indian presence in the state. Its title, *For as Long as the Waters Flow*, echoes the white man's often-repeated promise to set aside a permanent homeland expressly for the Indian—a place where he could remain his own master.

The Southern Cheyennes have also been involved in other, less public activities to commemorate their ancestral heritage. One of the most important and passionate issues of the day to Indian people is that of their ancestral bones that are being held by national universities, the Smithsonian Institution, and other museums. Non-Indians often fail to comprehend the intensity of Indian feeling on this matter.

The Cheyennes' deep, abiding respect for their ancestors has long been insulted by the callous disrespect that whites have shown for the remains of Indian dead. Graves of Indian dead have been dug up and robbed of peace medals, jewelry, and other artifacts. Bones have been left uncovered; and over the years other remains which have surfaced from flooding and wind erosion have been left unattended. Many have been carted off to museums and archives, supposedly for scientific examination.

A group known as the Sand Creek Cheyenne Descendants of Oklahoma is active in promoting the recovery of Cheyenne remains. The Southern Cheyennes are supported in this effort by the Northern Cheyennes. This state-certified group has undertaken a series of memorial events to honor their ancestral past. While their motivation is entirely spiritual, members hope that from these actions non-Indian people will begin to see the Indian side of the American experience.

In years past, numerous Indian skeletal parts have been unearthed in Oklahoma and often treated with indifference by white officials and citizens. The Cheyennes have been recovering those remains when possible and holding ceremonies of reburial. At the prompting of Sherman Goose, one set of bones was interred in the flag circle at the front of the Black Kettle Museum in Cheyenne, Oklahoma, on the one-hundredth anniversary of Custer's attack at the Washita.

Some have speculated that the bones are those of Black Kettle and his wife, but it is virtually certain that this is not true. Tribal accounts have it that the bodies of Black Kettle and his wife were recovered by members of his band after the battle and were buried at some unknown place away from the battlefield.

For many years another set of bones was kept on display in the window of the *Cheyenne News-Star* office at Cheyenne, Oklahoma, before eventually being discarded in the building's basement. They had been discovered in 1934 after flooding of the Washita had left them exposed in the river's bank. The basement was later cemented over, and the bones remained there until a new owner of the newspaper found them by accident.

This imposing statue of an Indian woman stands in front of the state Capitol building in Oklahoma City.

The Black Kettle Museum at Cheyenne, Oklahoma, contains Indian and military artifacts relating to Custer's massacre of Black Kettle's village in 1868.

In 1986 an article, in which the paper made light of the bones, came to the attention of John Sipes, Jr., a dedicated student of Cheyenne history. His great uncle Red Bird had been killed in the Washita attack. Sipes, whose Cheyenne name is Ah-in-nist or Red Tail Hawk, lost no time in writing to the *News-Star* to express his indignation at the article.

"The bones are very likely the skeletal remains of our Cheyenne ancestors," he wrote. "They should be treated with respect. They should also be given an honorable reburial."

As a result of Sipes' letter he was invited by the editor to pay him a visit and discuss the matter. In an amicable meeting the two agreed to having the bones interred near the battle site with a Cheyenne traditional burial ceremony.

On the afternoon of November 27, 1986, fifty-two years after their discovery, a small group of Cheyennes and others gathered in a pasture a mile west of Cheyenne, just a few hundred yards south of the Washita massacre site. They had come to rebury skeletal remains that had been examined earlier by Dr. Clyde Snow, world-famous forensic pathologist at the University of Oklahoma.

Dr. Snow identified the remains as being of an Indian male, forty-five to fifty years of age, and a younger woman, perhaps

John Sipes, Jr., and his wife, Dolores Subia Big Foot-Sipes, examine an Indian cradleboard with Bryce, Benita, and Beth Big Foot.

twenty-five to thirty at the time of her death. He determined that two large-caliber bullets had penetrated the left side of the male's skull. He had probably been shot at least once while lying on the ground. The skull of the female was incomplete, but Snow believed that she too had been shot in the head.

The wintry north wind stung the faces of the men as they carefully wrapped the two sets of human bones along with a token sprig of sage into separate Pendleton blankets. Each set was placed inside a wooden box and lowered into the grave that had been dug for them.

As they were covered with soil, the sound of a mournful memorial lament was carried off across the frozen hills by the prairie wind. Its undulating Indian cadence almost seemed to be an eerie call from the past as two long-dead victims of Custer's Washita attack finally received the honor of a tribal burial.

The burial group included Alfrich Heap of Birds, Keeper of the Sacred Medicine Arrows. His nephew, Hachivi Edgar Heap of Birds, who has been a state artist-in-residence at the University of Oklahoma, was a singer for the ceremony. Lucien Twin was the mourner. Others present included Bill Welge, archivist of the Oklahoma State Historical Society; Jim Briscoe, an archeological consultant; and Sipes.

There was no marker for the grave site, only a mound of red earth that would soon be lost among the prairie grass. Who the two people interred there were will never be known. But for the Cheyennes this was a symbolic rite representing more than merely the reburying of two deceased tribal members.

To Sipes and the other Cheyennes, it was a way of acknowledging all their people who perished not only at the Washita in 1868, but also Cheyennes killed at Sand Creek in 1864 and in the Palo Duro Canyon of the Texas Panhandle in 1874.

Descendants and friends, including an Indian military color guard, conduct a long overdue memorial service for Cheyenne scout Henry Standing Bird.

During the spring of 1990, an impressive ceremony was held to place a marker on the grave of former Cheyenne scout Henry Standing Bird, who had served with the U.S. Cavalry at Fort Reno during the 1880s—the man whom Agent Woodson had once praised for his advancement along the road of the white man.

The marker, provided by the Veterans Administration at the request of Sipes, Standing Bird's great-grandson, was installed at the scout's grave near Clinton. The small hilltop graveyard was marked by a single scrub-oak tree that stood silhouetted against the sky. By two o'clock on that warm spring afternoon, a small crowd had gathered to witness the event. Notable among them was an honor guard of Oklahoma Vietnam Intertribal Veterans.

The camouflage battle uniforms of these Indian-American warriors were bedecked with Vietnam unit patches and battle citations. The berets of some of the men bore feathers extending aslant at the back—the Cheyenne symbol of success in battle. Their presence lent an aura of martial dignity to the occasion. A color guard proudly displayed the U.S. and Oklahoma flags.

Following the reading of a short eulogy to Henry Standing Bird, Cheyenne Chief Laird Cometsevah led a traditional Cheyenne ritual in memory of the former scout. Flanked by a semicircle of six others who knelt facing the grave, the chief lit the ceremonial calumet. After saluting the four directions of the earth and wind, he passed the pipe among the group, each taking four symbolic puffs in turn.

A small depression was carefully prepared in the sandy soil before the chief. Now Cometsevah raised his hand above the hole and dropped into it an offering of food for the departed soul of the Cheyenne scout. Lyle Redbird poured the nourishment of water into the hole and two other participants came forward and with great care covered the offering with earth. This done, the group rose and stood with bowed heads as they joined Redbird in singing a Cheyenne lament to Standing Bird.

After the honor guard had fired twenty-one crisp volleys in salute to the dead scout, the ceremony was concluded with the presentation of the U.S. colors, under which Standing Bird had served, to his granddaughter, Cleo Sipes of Clinton.

▷ 8 ◁

A Renewal of Pride

THE CAUSES of defection from school by young Cheyennes and other Indian children are many. More than a few come from broken homes that barely manage to subsist on meager incomes well below the poverty line. They exist mostly on government commodities and what little money trickles down from the state and tribal governments. Additionally, the Indian youngster of small town Oklahoma suffers many of the same sociological barriers as faced by minority youths in the urban centers of America.

"Most of the problems of the Cheyennes begin with the problems of their children," notes Quentin Roman Nose, who has children of his own. "Modern education is important. But for these youngsters who live outside the main arena of society, education in self-worth is equally vital."

He believes strongly that the best way to help young Indians is to let them be as "Indian" as they wish. In line with this reasoning, Quentin and Larry Roman Nose are participants in the Cheyenne Children's Gourd Clan known as the "Circle Keepers." The organization was the idea of Cheyenne Christine George of Hammon, Oklahoma.

It is sponsored by the Cheyenne Cultural Center, Inc., and is co-directed by Chief Lawrence Hart, Director of Community Relations, and Joyce M. Twin, Director of Educational Services. The program seeks to educate and help Cheyennes from preschool age to age eighteen to remain drug and alcohol free.

The ultimate goal of its "Cheyenne Visions for 2001" program is for the four participating Oklahoma communities of Clinton, Hammon, Watonga, and Seiling to produce drug-free Cheyenne children by the start of the new century. The program is funded by the Robert Wood Johnson Foundation of the Johnson & Johnson Drug Company of Princeton, New Jersey, which does philanthropic work in health areas.

Youngsters pledge themselves to that goal upon becoming members of the community clans. Involvement of the parents and grandparents in this pledge to "remain healthy" is a critical factor in the program. The Cheyennes regard such pledges with great seriousness, and the young pledger is thus reinforced by family.

Further, Circle Keeper members undergo purification rites in a traditional Cheyenne sweat lodge. During this, they recite a petitionary or thanksgiving prayer. The youngsters also learn Cheyenne Gourd Clan songs, perform dramas, and take part in essay and other contests, including competition in the gourd dance itself.

Special uniforms are worn by the young gourd dancers: the girls a poly-cotton dress decorated with ribbons, a fringed red shawl, bead and bone chokers, hair ties, belts, leggings, and moccasins; the boys a poly-cotton shirt, red and blue blankets, dance beads, and shoulder sashes. One of their awards is a traditional Indian medicine (or perfume) bag of their own to wear attached to the sash at their back while dancing.

In his role as Indian counselor, Quentin Roman Nose has formed and sponsors the Watonga Indian Club. It is comprised of Indian children, some of whom are full-blooded Cheyennes or Arapahos, and some a mixture of the two or of other tribes and races.

Speakers are brought in to talk to them of their Indian heritage. Also, there are field trips, such as one recently to the Washita battlefield or another to the Oklahoma State Historical Society where the students could read about their ancestors in the old Indian records.

Recent essays by members of the Indian Club show that the program is making some progress. Mostly, the girls of the club expressed pride in their race and culture.

"I am proud of being Cheyenne and Arapaho," Regina Valentine Youngbear wrote. "I like to read and learn about our past."

"Cheyenne-Arapaho Indians are beautiful people," said Suzanne Whitebuffalo, a Cheyenne. "They are very spiritual in the Indian way . . . I wish more kids would get an education so the tribes would have a better future."

Michelle Johnson wrote that she was proud of her Cheyenne heritage, much of which she learned from her grandmother.

"I am proud to be Cheyenne and Arapaho," Betty Whiteshield stated. "I like carrying on the Whiteshield name."

"I would like to see more books written from the Indian's point of view," Becky Flynn insisted, "so that I, as an Indian, can identify with them and understand what they've gone through."

Members of the Watonga Indian Club include (above, left to right) Chiara
Greenhow, Cassandra Onco, Katy Flynn, and Gaylene Loneman; (below)
Loran Carter, left, and Regina Youngbear; (opposite) Maurisa Willis, left,
and Parry Roman Nose.

Chiara Greenhow, Katy Flynn, and Cassandra Onco told how they enjoyed dressing up in their pretty Indian costumes and attending the Cheyenne powwows and gourd dances.

Embedded in the essays by the boys of the club were traces of the old Cheyenne defiance. Donnie Beard remembers stories that his grandfather told him about his Cheyenne ancestors and how boys were trained to be brave. The young warriors fought and died to keep their land.

Parry Roman Nose said he wished that whites had never come to his land. Squire Weasel Bear, a Northern Cheyenne, declared that the Cheyennes were the best fighters and had a ceremony that helped overcome their enemies in war. His brother, Junior Weasel Bear, wished for two things: to get the Indians' land back and for whites to stop being so prejudiced.

"If God wanted me to be different," Adrienne Harjo proclaimed, "he would have made me somebody else . . . I wouldn't be here if there was no purpose for me in life."

But these are only a scant few of the Cheyenne and Arapaho student population. Even Quentin recognizes how little is being done to help the Indian youngsters and keep them in school. Under the Reagan administration, much of the federal help under programs such as Head Start and Outward Bound was reduced. Funds for the Title Five Indian Education Program were also cut back. As a result, many schools in the area with large Indian populations have no Indian counselors.

There is decreasing resistance within the tribal body over education and stepping out into the white man's world. More and more Cheyennes are going to college. Many have concluded that in order to compete with the white man, they must have a formal education. They feel they must become more aware economically, legally, and politically.

Some traditionalists, however, do not agree that a white man's education is the best for their children. Their determined detachment from white society is fueled by an ingrained resentment for past and present injustices. They feel that close association with the materialistic non-Indian world will inevitably contaminate and destroy the essence of being a Cheyenne, along with its strong inner values.

Traditionalist Terry Wilson also worried about the lack of interest among young Cheyennes in their heritage. Terry was initiated into the Cheyenne Bowstring Society when he was only fourteen years of age and began gourd dancing then. He has extensive background in the traditional ceremonies as a dancer, a Sun Dance priest, and a Sun Dance painter. He emphasizes that a man must have participated in four Sun Dances before he can paint others for the dance.

"There has been a great change during the past twenty or

thirty years," he claims. "Young people do not pay much attention to the Arrow ceremony."

He also blames the influence of white society, which has been strong through the effects of intermarriage and television. This has created a clash of cultures and leaves many young Indians confused.

Terry is deeply concerned over the loss of the Cheyenne language. He feels that Cheyenne traditions must be recorded and preserved. Being one of the few who still know the old Cheyenne songs, he undertook the taping of some of them for the University of Oklahoma oral history program. His concern is felt by many other Cheyennes.

"We must keep the prophecy of Sweet Medicine," Willie Fletcher insists, "and not lose our identity. If we lose our native language and tribal traditions, then we are lost as a people."

The issue of protecting native culture was addressed recently at the national level with Senate Bill S.1781, which has been signed into law. Its purpose, as stated, is:

> To establish as the policy of the United States the preservation, protection, and promotion of the rights of the Native Americans to use, practice, and develop Native American languages, to take steps to foster such use, practice, and development, and for other purposes.

The full ramification of this measure is not yet clear. Indian leaders in Oklahoma hope that it may lead to the teaching of Indian history, culture, and even language in the public schools. As yet the state has no teachers certified to teach Indian languages as does Wyoming.

However, some concerned Cheyennes and Arapahos are mov-

Marcianna Jacobs has done much to help disadvantaged urban Indian youths.

ing ahead on their own to resurrect their native tongues. Marcianna Littleman Jacobs, an energetic graduate of Chilocco Indian School, has taken it on herself to attack this problem. She has begun conducting Cheyenne language classes for Cheyenne children in Oklahoma City.

Marcianna has been working against great odds to help urban Indians in the city. As president of the Johnson-O'Malley Program Parent Committee, she has helped raise funds for clothing and other needs of children. Recently she persuaded the Cheyenne and Arapaho government to donate $1,000 to send Oklahoma City Indian children to attend an alcohol and substance abuse Awareness Camp at Stillwater. Another group attended summer classes on Indian culture at Oklahoma City's Southwest Junior College. They were provided money for transportation and meals.

Marcianna is also working to form a Cheyenne-Arapaho Urban Association. The aim of the group will be to raise funds to pay utility bills for urban Indians in need, buy food, finance school

Left: Cleo Sipes is justly proud of the moccasins which she makes by hand and beads in the Cheyenne traditional way.

Below: Larry Roman Nose of Watonga handcrafts and markets handsome beaded belts of Cheyenne design.

materials for students, and help with a variety of other needs. The organization will coordinate fund-raising measures such as garage sales, powwows, and Indian princess contests.

Another significant action undertaken by Marcianna has been to help organize a political support group among Cheyennes and Arapahos in the small towns of western Oklahoma. Called the Cheyenne and Arapaho Constitutional Compliance Committee, its aim is to institute political reforms in the tribal government. Through it, Marcianna hopes to secure equitable tribal funding for urban Indians, with special concern for the needs of children.

The movement reflects a new political activism by a younger, educated element of the Cheyennes that wishes to focus upon improving the lot of tomorrow's generation. Here they are in harmony with tribal traditionalists as they look to achieve their purpose through enhancement of their tribal heritage.

Other Cheyennes are working to carry on Cheyenne lore in traditional skills such as beading. Cleo Sipes specializes in making beaded moccasins and handbags, using Cheyenne methods she learned from her grandmother. She would love to pass her knowledge on to young Cheyenne girls, but most are either uninterested or too busy with other things.

Cleo's wares are sold all over the United States and in Europe, and many of them are purchased by tourists visiting the United States. These moccasins are each handmade and carefully stitched with nylon thread, as compared to the machine-produced imitations made in Taiwan and Hong Kong.

Cheyenne moccasins, she claims with much pride, are considered to be the most colorful and among the prettiest of all. Using carefully selected materials—just the right leather and the best beads—Cleo works out ancient Cheyenne designs. Most of the

Above: Janie Nightwalker of Thomas, Oklahoma, displays a Cheyenne ceremonial shield which she hand-crafted.

Left: Darrin West, son of Dana West of Kingfisher, Oklahoma, is a typical lively Cheyenne youngster.

images are taken from the world of nature, to which the Indian so closely relates.

Crosses on the moccasins represent the four directions of the wind that the Cheyennes traditionally recognize with their ceremonial pipes. The color of the beads has meaning, too. Red represents life, black death. Yellow is the bright daylight brought by the sun, blue is for the sky, and green is for the grass shoots of spring.

Dana West represents still another area in which Cheyenne tradition is endangered. As a licensed funeral director, he is one of the few who knows the traditional ceremony for tribal burials. No one has a higher respect for the dead than the Cheyennes.

"In the old days we placed our loved ones on scaffolds or in trees," Dana observed, "returning later to gather and bury their bones with a traditional ceremony. We no longer follow this procedure, of course. And many of our practices of burial dress, mourning, and funeral procedures are being lost to commercial funeral directing."

Still, Cheyenne funerals, much honored events, are distinctive of their tribal culture. Once the body has been readied for burial, it is taken back to the family's home where a wake is held. Much food is brought by friends, who join the family in singing Cheyenne songs and giving prayers through the night.

A ceremonial dinner will be held in keeping with the Cheyenne tradition of feeding the spirit with the staples of meat, liquid, something sweet, and fry bread. The bereaved family may request that the tribal traditionalists present take a full portion of the meat.

The church service, usually conducted by a Cheyenne pastor, will often be delivered in both Cheyenne and English and feature Cheyenne hymns. And at the end, the unique "give-away" of gifts to the family and those participating in the burial ceremony will be held. When the casket is lowered into the grave, songs are sung that are appropriate, according to whether the deceased is a chief, a headman, a member of a warrior society, or a veteran.

Like other Indian tribes, the Cheyennes look to their problems with much concern, but also with great resolve. They are determined to preserve the essence of their tribal existence against the enormous pressures of a rapidly changing world. At the same time, they and other tribes are working to enhance the public appreciation for Indian culture.

Both Justice Kauger and Linda Skinner, Director of Indian Education for the State of Oklahoma, cite instances where white children have responded with great delight at the presentation of Indian dances and other cultural events.

"In truth," Skinner notes, "those schools which do nothing to invite such performances are overlooking an important educational medium, as well as a vital link between the Indian and white world."

▷ 9 ◁

Warriors with Portfolios

DURING THE nineteenth century and before, the Indian warrior's main responsibility was protection of his people. His weapons were the knife, the bow and arrow, the tomahawk, and the gun. He was fierce, wily, and relentless in defense of his land—none more so than the Cheyenne. The image of the Indian fighter is as sharp against the backdrop of history as that of the Viking raider, the Roman legionnaire, the English longbowman, or the French cavalier.

Today the Indian warrior is fighting to protect his people with a new kind of weapon. Now he employs the weapons of words, arguments, legal interpretations, and legislative persuasion to safeguard tribal rights. The modern tribesman or tribeswoman may carry a briefcase, and in it weapons such as treaty documents, governmental acts, legal writs, or even a painting or poem that gives expression to the Indian viewpoint.

There has emerged from the modern Indian tribe a new breed of well-educated, articulate spokespersons—Indian men and women who more and more are stepping forth to demand the rights of their people and the correction of old wrongs. Prominent Indian leaders and intellectuals from around the entire nation have met for the past three years at the annual Sovereignty Symposium sponsored by the Oklahoma Supreme Court and Oklahoma Indian Affairs Commission.

This legal symposium provides Indians with an opportunity to exchange ideas with both state and federal jurists concerning legal issues in a scholarly, nonhostile environment. The issues concern tribal agreements, criminal law, gaming, land titles, tribal courts, fishing rights, environmental law, Indian child welfare, taxation, international problems, and other areas of vital importance to Indians.

Twenty-nine-year-old Nathan Hart typifies the new formally educated Indian who is today emerging more and more upon the American scene. A graduate of Bethel College in Kansas, with postgraduate work at the University of Oklahoma, he has worked as a business development specialist, served as vice president of a security brokerage firm, and is now Director of the Oklahoma Indian Affairs Commission.

Handsome, smartly dressed in suit and tie at work, Hart fits well the image of a young American business executive. At the same time, he is a Cheyenne traditionalist. He has been gourd dancing since high school and recently participated in his first Sun Dance. He also performs as a dancer, dressed in full costume as he is shown on the jacket of this book.

Hart believes strongly in the traditions of his people, but just as strongly in the value of education for his people. "The Indian

Nathan Hart, Director of the Oklahoma Indian Affairs Commission

Cheyenne W. Richard West was named as the first Director of the Smithsonian's National Museum of the American Indian in Washington, D.C.

today," he observes, "must realize that this is a new era. He still must fight to maintain tribal traditions, identity, and sovereignty, just as in the old days. But now he does combat in the legal and economic spheres. For that, he must prepare himself through education."

There are more and more Southern Cheyennes who overcome these barriers to the mainstream of American life and prove their ability to compete and achieve success in the white man's world. Only recently W. Richard West, a Southern Cheyenne lawyer from Muskogee, Oklahoma, was appointed to the highly regarded position of Director of the Smithsonian Institution's National Museum of the American Indian in Washington, D.C.

Connie Hart, daughter of Lawrence and Betty Hart of Clinton and sister to Nathan, is a practicing attorney at Albuquerque, New Mexico. After earning an M.A. degree in history from Purdue University, she graduated from the Oklahoma City University Law School. Connie served as a district judge for the Cheyenne and Arapaho District Court for a year before leaving to fulfill a commitment in the office of a federal judge.

Susan Shawn Harjo is president and director of the Morning Star Foundation, a nonprofit organization for American Indian cultural rights. During the Carter administration, she served as special assistant in the office of the Secretary of the Interior. She was also executive director of the National Congress of American Indians. Kathryn Bell is managing editor for the *Intertribal*, a journal serving Oklahoma's Indian community-at-large.

Dr. Henrietta Whiteman is still another Cheyenne woman who has traveled far from her home at Hammon in western Oklahoma to become a professor of Indian Studies at the University of Montana. Henrietta, whose ancestors were victimized at both Sand Creek and the Washita, rose above the prejudice of her community and school to earn her doctorate at the University of New Mexico.

Lance Henson is a Southern Cheyenne who has proven that even a Cheyenne youngster from a small Oklahoma town can find worldwide recognition for his talents. Lance has been a lecturer, teacher, and poet-in-residence at more than five hundred schools and universities in the U.S. and Europe.

These include such prestigious institutions as New York University, Oberlin, UCLA, Iowa State, Kansas University, the German universities of Mainz and Osnabrück, and many others in Italy, Austria, Denmark, Sweden, Luxembourg, and Yugoslavia.

Lance was raised on his grandparents' allotment near Calumet, just west of Oklahoma City. After serving in Vietnam with the U.S. Marines, Lance went on to college, earning his bachelor's and master's degrees in English and Creative Writing. He is a member of both the modern Black Belt Karate Association and the ancient Cheyenne Dog Soldier warrior society.

To date, Lance has published twelve books of poetry, several of which have received special acclaim. Though he now resides in Albany, New York, with his family, the bonds of his Cheyenne heritage are unbreakable. A strong activist on Indian and environmental issues, he seldom misses the opportunity to attend the Cheyenne Arrow Renewal and Sun Dance.

Another Cheyenne success story is Hachivi Edgar Heap of Birds, a direct descendant of the Suhtai chief, Heap of Birds. Born and raised in a Cheyenne environment, he was intimate from infancy with the throb of dance drums and smell of sweet grass burning, and he came to know the full meaning and moral power of the tipi circle.

After graduating from high school, where he revealed special art talents, he attended the Tyler School of Art in Philadelphia, receiving his M.F.A. there. Later he studied at the Royal College of Art in London, England.

Heap of Birds has also served as a visiting lecturer in art at Yale University, the Whitney Museum Independent Studies Program in New York City, the California Institute of Arts, and the University of Ulster in Belfast. In 1989 he was awarded the National Arts Award of the Tiffany Foundation in New York.

The works of this Cheyenne artist utilize a broad range of modern communication: drawings, prints, paintings, and textual messages expressed through posters, billboards, and digital signs. His themes have been intellectual, social, and political. In particular, they address the Indians' struggle for equal coexistence in their native land.

One writer observed that Heap of Birds' "message is a fact of American history that has been hidden from our American conscience." Another made note of his efforts "to rebuild the strength and self-confidence of native peoples."

There are many other excellent and successful Cheyenne artists working to portray and preserve the Cheyenne existence on canvas. Among the most noted are Dick West, Sr., who now resides in New Mexico; traditional Chief Archie Blackowl, of Cushing, Oklahoma; and Benny Buffalo of Norman.

Some Cheyenne latter-day warriors work independently, and some with appropriate organizations. Others operate within the framework of tribal governments, such as the Cheyenne and Arapaho Tribal Council. The Cheyenne system of forty-four chiefs, with four of them being head chiefs, still exists. Today, however, tribal business affairs are managed by an elected Board of Directors and a Chairperson for the combined Cheyenne and Arapaho tribes. The Board's headquarters are located at Concho, a few miles north of El Reno.

Much is being done with the tribal government by professional people to encourage and assist young Indians to advance their education beyond the public schools. The tribes provide assistance for both college or university education and technical training. A Head Start school is conducted at Concho for Cheyenne and Arapaho youngsters.

An astute executive, Tom Burns oversees the granting and obtaining of scholarships for Cheyenne and Arapaho young people. The tribes will fund up to five years of higher education at accredited institutions in Oklahoma, as long as the student maintains a two-point grade average on a full-time basis.

"One difficulty we face," Burns noted, "is the old-fashioned thinking by some college officials who believe the tribes can still pay the entire cost of a student's education. The result is that they reject applications by Indians for financial aid."

Out-of-state tuition is usually prohibitive to the limited funds available to the tribes. Special consideration is given when a particular educational program is not offered in the state. Ten percent of the tribal educational fund is set aside for graduate work.

Burns and his department also work closely with colleges and universities in procuring educational grants, work-study assistance, and other financial aids. These are often needed to help students from financially distressed families with extra college costs.

Indian students can also attend one of three schools operated by the Bureau of Indian Affairs: Haskell Institute in Kansas, Southwestern Indian Polytech Institute in Albuquerque, or the Institute of American Indian Arts in Santa Fe.

Many young Indians prefer the all-Indian schools where they feel more comfortable socially. These schools also work with Indian students who come from small towns where the curriculum is limited.

Most of the larger colleges and universities have Indian counselors who help Indian students with their social and academic problems. Churches have developed groups to aid them as well.

The tribal government offers financial and other assistance for attending vocational schools that offer a wide variety of technical skills. The tribal member must reside within the area of the former Cheyenne-Arapaho reservation to qualify.

Fred Mosqueda, an Arapaho, is in charge of this program at Concho, which also provides job placement assistance. He points proudly to the fact that during the past year's time 144 tribal members were placed in jobs.

However, he also stresses that the discouraging reality is that many Indian youths do not stick with employment. There are a number of factors which contribute to this.

"Almost all the jobs are away from home," Mosqueda observed. "Young Indians are very shy and uncomfortable away from home. There is an old saying that sixteen miles is the limit for an Indian to stray from home. Beyond that, he comes back. Also, the Indian is the last to be hired, and the first fired."

As a result, many young Indians return home, where they often fall into habits of alcoholism and drug use. A new program called Job Opportunity and Basic Skills, or JOBS, has been developed by the tribes. Modeled after the state program, it seeks to train alcohol and drug center clients who are on welfare and get them working.

An important political effort is presently being made by the

Cheyenne and Arapaho tribes. Led by Cheyenne-Arapaho Tribal Chairman Eddie Wilson, the Tribal Council is engaged in an effort to regain control of the land that constitutes old Fort Reno military reservation. Located just north of El Reno, the fort is on land originally taken from the Cheyenne and Arapaho reservation area.

Former Chairperson Juanita Learned and others have made several trips to Washington, D.C., to meet with Senator Daniel K. Inouye, chairman of the Senate Select Committee on Indian Affairs, and other congressional members on the matter.

"We want the title of Fort Reno," Learned states, "to be held by the Department of Interior in trust for the Cheyenne and Arapaho tribes. Our goal is to preserve the fort and utilize the lands for the economic and educational development of our people." There is also the hope of creating a historical museum and archives that would be of great value as a research center and tourist attraction.

A Cheyenne winter camp near Fort Reno, Oklahoma, in 1890. Land for old Fort Reno was taken from the Cheyenne-Arapaho reservation.

The Southern Cheyenne and Arapaho reservation was established by executive order of President Ulysses S. Grant on August 10, 1869. During the Cheyenne uprising of 1874, U.S. troops camped south of Darlington Agency on a site where Fort Reno was founded the following year within the reservation area.

In 1883, 6,900 acres of the Cheyenne-Arapaho reservation surrounding the post were set apart for a military reserve. Finally abandoned as a garrison in 1908, it was used as a remount station until 1949. The U.S. cavalry kept large numbers of horses and mules there.

During the active days of Fort Reno, Cheyenne and Arapaho scouts joined both white and black cavalry units (the black troopers were called "buffalo soldiers" by the Indians) in military action against hostile Plains bands and patrolling against illicit whiskey traders in western Oklahoma. These units were also used during the 1880s to eject David L. Payne's "Oklahoma boomers," who were agitating to open the country to white settlement with invasion tactics.

The U.S. Tenth Circuit Court has ruled that tribal lands remaining after the Cheyenne-Arapaho reservation was disestablished in 1891 were held in trust for the tribes. The Cheyenne-Arapaho tribes have received strong support from Senator Inouye. After several meetings with tribal officials, Inouye recently contacted the U.S. Department of the Interior for a legal opinion on the merit of the tribes' claim to Fort Reno, which he felt was substantial.

The Department responded that if the fort lands were to be declared excess federal property, they would satisfy the requirements of the Surplus Property Act of 1982. This potentially left the matter in the hands of the U.S. Congress.

Fort Reno has since been used by the Department of Agriculture as an experiment station and is presently under its control. A unique aspect of the fort area is a burial ground for German prisoners of war who were held there during World War II.

The tribal claim, however, has come under challenge from a non-Indian El Reno group which organized as the Friends of Fort Reno. This group has proposed that a coalition be formed to manage a 300-acre "support area" of the fort as a history-oriented tourist attraction. The suggested coalition would be comprised of representatives from the Friends of Fort Reno, the Cheyenne and Arapaho tribes, the city of El Reno, the El Reno Chamber of Commerce, and other historical, governmental, and civic groups.

The group has gained the support of Oklahoma's state and national legislative leaders. This has seriously inhibited the efforts of the tribe and Senator Inouye. The Senator has indicated, however, that if legislative efforts fail, he and the tribe may turn to the federal executive administration.

▷ **10** ◁

Reconciliation on
the Smoky Hill

IS IT POSSIBLE for two divergent races who fought a violent, bloody war with one another to find eventually a common ground of understanding and friendship?

A significant act toward that end took place on September 9, 1990, on the Smoky Hill River of western Kansas. There descendants of Cheyenne and white families, both of whom had had innocent ancestors killed during the Plains Indian wars, embraced and took part in a ceremony of peace and good will.

This peace ceremony evolved out of one of the bloody events of the Plains Indian wars. The incident occurred in the fall of 1874. It was then that the family of John German was traveling west through western Kansas on its way to Colorado. The former Georgia family consisted of John, his wife, Liddia, and their seven children, Rebecca, Stephen, Joanna, Catherine, Sophia, Julia, and Nancy.

They had just broken camp along the Smoky Hill River on the morning of September 11 when they were attacked by fifteen Cheyenne Bowstring Society warriors and two Cheyenne women under Chief Medicine Water. The family evidently had no realization that it was traveling through a war zone, that western Kansas was still being fiercely contested by the Cheyennes against an unending flood of whites.

John German, Liddia, Rebecca, Stephen, and Joanna were killed by the Cheyennes, and the four young girls, ranging from four years of age to sixteen, were taken off into captivity. The captive girls were held until the following spring. Then pressure from U.S. troops finally forced the beleaguered and starving Cheyennes to surrender. Upon her release, twelve-year-old Sophia German pointed out a Cheyenne woman named Buffalo Calf Woman as being the one who had killed her mother with an axe.

Calf Woman's act was nothing less than murderous, but there is another side to Calf Woman's story, which is often overlooked. She and her family had been in Black Kettle's village at Sand Creek when Chivington made his undeniably brutal attack. The atrocities committed there by white soldiers equaled or surpassed those often charged against Indians.

"I did not see a body of man, woman, or child but was scalped," 1st Lt. James Cannon testified under oath concerning Sand Creek. "And in many instances their bodies were mutilated in the most horrible manner . . . I heard of one instance of a child a few months old being thrown in the feedbox of a wagon, and after being carried some distance left on the ground to perish."

He stated also that one man had cut the heart out of an Indian woman and carried it about on a stick. Cpl. Amos C. Miksch said that he saw a little Indian boy covered up among dead bodies in a trench, still alive. An officer took out his pistol and blew off the top of the child's head.

Calf Woman, then twenty-three years old, had been among those who managed to escape. She was the only member of her family to survive the attack. Like others, she fled north to a Cheyenne campsite known as the "Bunch of Trees" on Cherry Creek in northwestern Kansas. The weather was bitterly cold. Most of the people had no robes or even moccasins, and many had been wounded by the soldiers' bullets or sabers.

Like the Cheyenne warriors, Calf Woman swore revenge. She took up a rifle and became a warrior-woman alongside her husband, Medicine Water. She considered herself to be at war when she participated in the massacre of the German family.

When they were captured, both Calf Woman and Medicine Water were placed in chains and sent with other Cheyennes to Fort Marion, Florida. They were confined in prison there for three years. Afterward both returned to their reservation area in western Oklahoma where they lived out the remainder of their lives in peace.

The 1990 reunion of descendants came about as a result of correspondence between the great-granddaughter of Sophia German, Arlene Jauken of Troutdale, Oregon, and the great-great-grandson of Calf Woman, John Sipes, who worked as a researcher for the Oklahoma Historical Society.

During an amicable exchange of letters and phone calls, the two descendants agreed to meet at the site of the massacre eight miles northwest of Russell Springs, Kansas. When citizens who lived in the area learned of this, they made plans to enhance the affair.

The German Family-Cheyenne Peace Ceremonial Commis-

Henry Roman Nose, Yellow Bear, and Lame Man were among Southern Cheyennes held prisoner at Fort Marion, Florida.

sion was formed at Russell Springs through the efforts of Leslie Linville, author-historian of Colby, Kansas, and Capt. M. L. Baughn, president of the Russell Springs Butterfield Trail Association.

The 7th Cavalry Drill Team of Fort Wallace, Kansas, participated in the ceremony. This unit, under Col. Gary LaGrange, is a modern re-creation of the old 7th Cavalry as it was during the days of the Indian wars. Newspapers in Nebraska, Colorado, and Kansas gave extensive coverage to the event.

In conjunction with the descendants' peace meeting, a ceremony was held on September 8 at the old Cheyenne campsite on Cherry Creek near St. Francis, Kansas. It was there in the aftermath of the Sand Creek Massacre that Cheyenne survivors of Black Kettle's village had taken refuge during the winter of 1864–1865.

This was the place, too, where the Cheyenne Dog Soldiers had organized for war after Sand Creek. Supported by the Arapahos and Sioux, they conducted a retaliatory raid against Julesburg, Colorado, and nearby Fort Rankin in early January, 1865, as the start of a general war of vengeance.

Through a cooperative effort by the St. Francis Chamber of Commerce, the High-Plains Historical Society, and the Fort Wallace Memorial Society, memorials to the victims of Sand Creek were erected at the Cherry Creek site. These memorials were in the form of iron sculptures depicting an Indian tipi, an Indian on horseback, a buffalo, a rabbit, and a prairie dog.

During the Cherry Creek meeting, Cleo Sipes presented a pair of Cheyenne moccasins which she had made to the sculptor of the memorials, Tobe Zweygardt of St. Francis. John Sipes conducted a traditional Cheyenne peace ceremony, during which he puffed smoke to the four directions of the wind in the ancient way of his people.

On the next day, an estimated 850 people from twenty states, some as far away as California, Oregon, and Wisconsin, attended the peace ceremony on the Smoky Hill. They were descendant family members, historically active people, and others who were simply intrigued by this unique reconciliation of white and Indian people. Many of those present were curious regarding the attitude of present-day Cheyennes to the German attack.

As master of ceremonies, Baughn introduced Arlene Jauken, who had known her great-grandmother, Sophia German Feldman, before she died. She told of stories that she had heard from her great-grandmother concerning her six months in captivity—how

Cheyenne and white descendants of the German family massacre meet in reconciliation 126 years later on the Smoky Hill River of western Kansas.

Sophia and her sisters had been traded about for horses, how they had almost starved because the Cheyennes had little food, how her moccasins had frozen to her feet during the winter. Mrs. Jauken still had one of the moccasins.

She ended her talk by saying:

"Today, I would like to say peace to the Cheyenne people and to five generations of the German family. To fight each other would merely mean to fight ourselves."

Sipes responded in kind, stressing that the reunion meant a great deal to him.

"I hope that from this," he said, "everyone will have a better understanding and know that the barriers to harmonious relations between the races can be removed."

He said that as a youngster, he, too, had listened to gruesome stories—stories of his ancestors who were slaughterd and butchered with sabers at Sand Creek.

"I have researched the testimony on it," Sipes noted, "and it was depressing. Then I studied the German massacre. That wasn't a pretty sight, either. That was depressing, too.

"I hope we all leave here with a better understanding of the Cheyenne ways and the non-Indian ways."

The extraordinary spirit of conciliation in this meeting reached Washington, D.C. It was reflected in a letter that the participants received from the president of the United States, George Bush. He wrote:

Dear Friends:

I am delighted to send greetings to the descendants of John German and those of Medicine Water and Calf Woman as you gather at the peace ceremonial and reunion.

By coming together in this way, you are setting a wonderful example of peace and forgiveness for yourselves and for future generations. As the German Family-Cheyenne Peace Ceremonial Commission sets aside 116 years of painful recriminations, Barbara and I hope that this gathering will also be the beginning of future reconciliation for the family members.

No one wants better relations between the whites and Indians more than the Cheyennes. Except when driven to war, they historically have tried to live in peace and harmony. But complete reconciliation has not yet come. There still remain significant obstacles to racial harmony and improvement in the Southern Cheyennes' condition.

The biases and unfair treatment exercised at times by white people, the latent distrust of whites by Cheyennes, and the difficult adjustments between their tribal traditions and the modern world are problems that are yet to be overcome.

The answer, many Cheyennes feel, lies in the recognition and acceptance of Indian culture by the white majority and in the freedom for Cheyenne youngsters to participate in American society with a sense of self-pride and belonging—as citizens and as Indians.

Selected Bibliography

Ashabranner, Brent. *Morning Star, Black Sun*. New York: Putnam Publishing Group (Dodd, Mead), 1982.

Berthrong, Donald J. *The Cheyenne and Arapaho Ordeal*. Norman: University of Oklahoma Press, 1976.

———. *The Southern Cheyennes*. Norman: University of Oklahoma Press, 1963.

Grinnell, George Bird. *The Cheyenne Indians: Their History and Ways of Life*. 2 vols. New Haven: Yale University Press, 1923.

———. *The Fighting Cheyennes*. Norman: University of Oklahoma Press, 1956.

Hoebel, E. Adamson. *The Cheyennes: Indians of the Great Plains*. New York: Rinehart and Winston, 1960.

Hoig, Stan. *The Battle of the Washita: The Sheridan-Custer Indian Campaign of 1867-69*. New York: Doubleday, 1976.

————. *The Cheyenne*. (The Indians of North America Series). New York: Chelsea House Publishers, 1989.

————. *The Peace Chiefs of the Cheyennes*. Norman: University of Oklahoma Press, 1980.

————. *The Sand Creek Massacre*. Norman: University of Oklahoma Press, 1961.

Hyde, George E. *Life of George Bent: Written from His Letters*. Norman: University of Oklahoma Press, 1987.

Llewellyn, Karl N. and E. Adamson Hoebel. *The Cheyenne Way*. Norman: University of Oklahoma Press, 1941.

Moore, John H. *The Cheyenne Nation: A Social and Demographic History*. pap. University of Nebraska Press, 1987.

Ottoway, Harold Nelson. "The Cheyenne Arrow Ceremony." Thesis, Wichita State University, Wichita, Kansas, 1969.

Penoi, Charles. *No More Buffaloes*. Yukon, Oklahoma: Pueblo Publishing Press, 1981.

Powell, Peter J. *Sweet Medicine*. 2 vols. Norman: University of Oklahoma Press, 1969.

Index